RH

NINE HANDSOME MISSOURI BOYS

—who walked into a bullet-whistling hell and came out with grain sacks full of cash.

—who made love in the darnedest places, but had a hard time staying around.

—who lived life to the hilt at every moment, because any moment could be their last.

D1560303

THE LONG RIDERS

a novel by

STEVEN PHILLIP SMITH

based on the screenplay by

William Bryden
Steven Phillip Smith and
Stacy & James Keach

AVON
PUBLISHERS OF BARD, CAMELOT AND DISCUS BOOKS

AVON BOOKS
A division of
The Hearst Corporation
959 Eighth Avenue
New York, New York 10019

First Avon Printing, June, 1980

For Walter Hill
with appreciation

ya kon vas nog

1

Jacob Rixley knew it was a time for happiness. He knew he should have been out with his boys, pleasantly drunk and whooping it up, going over the chase and the kill, and feeling satisfied about accomplishing his mission. But his boys were all dead, and he preferred solitude to the company of the swine whom he'd had to enlist to accomplish his famous mission. He'd drunk half a bottle of whiskey by himself, but the booze tasted rotten and served only to heighten his fatigue. He sat in the far corner of a Missouri saloon, his back to the door, and he felt neither fear nor curiosity as he listened to the tread of boots approach his table and stop.

"Mr. Rixley?"

The voice had a quiet dignity, a quality that Rixley had not heard much lately. "That's right." He watched the amber fluid swirling in his glass.

"My name's Frank James."

Rixley set down his glass and stared at it, half expecting to have his brains spilled on the scarred wood of the table. Then he turned slowly and looked up.

"I'd like to surrender to you," Frank said. "Give you my gun." He held the gleaming barrel in his hand and slowly extended his arm until the rich wooden pistol butt was only a foot from Rixley's face. "In return I want to bury my brother."

Jacob Rixley, Pinkerton man, fought an impulse to reach out and grab the famous outlaw's gun. He felt an absurd desire to shake Frank James' hand and invite him

7

to sit down for a drink. He stared at the brown mustache, then into the large determined eyes, and he knew that Frank James was serious and that his offer was reasonable. Still, Mr. Rixley had grown used to bargaining, and he found that the habit did not easily leave him. "Suppose I don't agree to your terms?" He felt a moment's pride that his voice betrayed no fear.

Frank James withdrew his gun, returned the butt to his hand, and cocked the hammer. Now it was the barrel of the gun that wavered ever so slightly before Rixley's face. "I'll kill you."

Rixley did not doubt him, and for the first time that evening a smile creased his normally taciturn face. "Mr. James," he said, "you have the advantage." Frank's nod was barely perceptible. "You also have my word. You see, I'm as tired of this chase as you are." Rixley turned back to the table and took another sip of whiskey. For once it warmed him going down. He stared at the table as Frank carefully placed the revolver next to the bottle.

"My God," Rixley said. "You're gonna outlive 'em all."

2

Frank James may have hated the railroads, but he flat out loved trains. He'd had his good times robbing them, and even now he looked back on the fateful Pullman ride to Minnesota with pleasure. He'd ridden like a gentleman, reading the newspaper and occasional verses of scripture, and swapping bits of outlaw philosophy and reminiscences about Quantrill with his old friend Cole Younger. Well, Cole was in for life at the Stillwater penitentiary with his brothers Jim and Bob, and Frank was probably going to do a nice long stint himself. Frank moved his arm slightly, and the manacle that bound him to Jacob Rixley tightened. With his other hand Frank tipped his hat to a group of people standing near the edge of the woods, people who'd come out to pay respects as the funeral train of Jesse James rolled by.

Frank and Rixley stood in the open doorway of the baggage car, Jesse's coffin behind them. "You'd think we were carrying Abraham Lincoln," Rixley said, "the way people have been coming out to see the train and all."

"If it was Lincoln there wouldn't be so many." Frank looked at Rixley and shrugged. "Those people thought Jesse was fighting for them."

Rixley shook his head. "I've learned that, chasing you fellows through half the hills of Missouri."

"You're all finished now," Frank said.

Rixley nodded. "Sure am."

9

"You can go back to Chicago and forget about all these sodbusters and hillbillies."

"Ain't life grand?" Rixley said. He watched the fleeting landscape for a moment, then turned again to Frank. "All that stuff about you fighting the banks and railroads. Was there ever anything to it?"

Frank eyed him, saying nothing.

"Really," Rixley said. "It'll be just between us."

"Hell," Frank said. "I don't know. If there was it sure got lost somewhere along the way. I never believed it much myself, and I don't reckon Cole Younger did either. I can't speak for the others."

Rixley nodded at the coffin behind them. "What about your brother?"

"Oh, he believed it," Frank said. "That was his problem. He always thought he was doin' more than he was really doin'. Probably a lot of men in the history books just like that. Seems to me that a leader usually makes use of other men's ideas, you know what I mean?"

Rixley nodded.

"That's the way Jesse was with Cole, and I think that's why there was always that edge between 'em. That's the way we got started, and that's the way we ended, and things wasn't always that smooth in between."

"Tell me about it," Rixley said.

Both Jesse James and Coleman Younger had gone back to farming after the Civil War. Jesse was restless, but all his extra energy went into his farm chores. Cole farmed for three months, then just disappeared. He showed up half a year later, and he took Jesse James for a little walk through the wheat field.

"So what the hell you been up to the past few months?" Jesse asked. Cole wouldn't say a word to him until they got away from everyone else.

"This and that." Cole put something into Jesse's hand. "I brung you a present."

Jesse James unfolded the bill and stared at it in amazement. "A hundred-dollar bill! Where'd you get that kind of money?"

Cole gestured at the surrounding field. "Growin' out of the ground like wheat."

"Wheat my ass!" Jesse said. "Where'd you get it?"

"Buy yourself a new suit," Cole said.

Jesse thumped his forehead and began to laugh. "You robbed the goddam bank." He pointed at Cole. "I read the paper, but I never figured you for it."

Cole just smiled.

"Must've been like old times," Jesse said, a nostalgic look passing over his face. "Must've been like ridin' with Quantrill."

Cole shook his head. "Quantrill's dead. War's over."

"They were some times, though."

"Ain't no old times, Jesse. Old times is dead times. The only times there is is new times."

"What's happening tomorrow."

Cole nodded. "That's right." He handed Jesse three more hundred-dollar bills.

"I believe it," Jesse said. "I believe I see a whole new day comin'." He burst out laughing.

"Want to talk to your brother?" Cole asked.

"Think he might be real interested," Jesse said.

Jesse and Cole found Frank in the saloon, studying the newspaper with a glass of whiskey in front of him. Cole leaned on the bar while Jesse harangued Frank about their new economic opportunity, but Frank, already mellow with drink at three in the afternoon, didn't seem that enthusiastic. Finally Jesse slammed his palm on the bar. "Frank, it's a damn good idea, and it's time for us to move."

"It's awful sudden," Frank said. "I need some more time to think."

"Well," Jesse said, "I'll tell you what. I had enough of plowin' and shovelin' shit and lookin' for eggs."

"Farming's not so bad."

Jesse laughed in Frank's face. "Then what you doin' suckin' up whiskey in the afternoon? Every afternoon." Jesse paused a moment to let his words sink in. "You ain't no farmer, and if you are you're a piss-poor one. I'm missin' the war, Frank. It'll be like ridin' with Quantrill again. It's what I'm trained for." He looked at Cole, then back at Frank. "I'm gonna organize some men. The Youngers—"

"I handle the Youngers," Cole said.

Jesse turned to Cole. "You think Bob's ready?"

"I'll be the one that worries it," Cole said.

"How about Ed and Clell Miller?" Jesse asked.

"I don't know about them two." Cole signaled the bartender for a drink.

"You handle the Youngers," Jesse said. "I'll handle the Millers." He eyed Cole, who simply shook his head.

"Maybe I ought to listen a little more to all this," Frank said. "It's startin' to sound pretty interesting."

Jesse grinned and slapped him on the back. "We might fit you in somewhere."

"Might be like old times," Frank said.

"There ain't no old times, Frank," Jesse said. "Only thing there is is new times. You got to learn that."

Cole Younger held his tongue and drank his whiskey.

The next thing Jesse James did was call an organizational meeting. He thought that coming late might be a good idea—that way he could ride in and call the men to order. The other men, all eager to leave their labors in the fields for more lucrative pursuits, arrived early, and they managed to put away Ed Miller's bottle of whiskey in forty-five minutes. They lounged beneath the big oak tree at the side of Dunham's Livery Stable, Ed Miller and Jim Younger providing the entertainment by arm wrestling on a tree stump.

"Come on, Jim," Cole said. "You best protect the family name." He looked across the way at Ed's brother. "Otherwise I'm gonna have to whip old Clell here."

"That's a caboose full of shit too," Clell Miller said.

Ed's and Jim's arms remained locked in the upright position. "When I get through with your brother," Ed grunted, "he won't even remember his name."

Bob Younger sneaked up behind Ed and suddenly bellowed into his ear. Jim slammed the back of Ed's hand onto the stump.

"Another victory for the Youngers," Bob crowed.

"Youngers are shit," Ed Miller said bitterly. "Can't win without cheatin'."

"I'll show you who's shit." Bob Younger raised his fists and menaced Ed with a bucktoothed leer.

"Before you boys fall on the ground with one another, maybe we better go over a few notions."

Everyone turned away from Bob and Ed to see Jesse sitting on his horse. He looked at them all, then dismounted. He suddenly drew both pistols from his shoulder holsters, took aim at a small wagon full of melons across the road, and fired four times. Four melons exploded. He faced the men again. "Cole told me how a few boys got drunk and robbed the bank over to Fayette. Y'all got anything to say to that?"

"Good on you, Cole." Ed Miller took careful aim with his rifle and obliterated a melon of his own.

Clell picked up his rifle and aimed at the wagon. "Can't argue with takin' their money." He blew away three melons.

A few townspeople, mainly kids, gathered near the livery stable to watch the shooting.

"Anything strike you as, uh, improvable about the way they done it?" Jesse asked.

Cole stared at Jesse while Jim took out two melons with his Winchester.

"Cole's damn lucky to still have his hide," Jesse said. "You get a bunch of drunks shootin' up a town, and somebody's bound to get it."

"Don't be pickin' on the Youngers," Bob said.

"Shut up, Bob," Jim said.

"Aw, shit!" Bob fanned his revolver and destroyed five more melons.

"Yeah," Cole said. "Shut up, Bob boy."

"I ain't pickin'," Jesse said. "But the hardest thing about a robbery is makin' a plan. You need friends for after, people that'll hide you as if nothin' had happened. You don't get kindness from folks by killin' their kids."

"It was accidental," Cole said.

"Accidental or not," Jesse said, "he was a boy of no more than fifteen. Mighta been the only support of his mother."

"You know everything, Jesse." Cole aimed his rifle and destroyed a melon. "I'm just the fella that robbed the bank."

"I'll say my piece, Cole. Then each of us can vote free."

"Let's hear ya, Jesse," Jim said. "Just be right."

"It's like we're all kin," Jesse said. "No one's gonna hand over another to any laws. Seven people. We ride the best mounts available. And we only kill a fella when he's riskin' our own lives. Like Quantrill told us, 'Think about what you're doin' when you're doin' it, so afterward you ain't sorry or dead.' "

"Seems to me Quantrill's dead," Cole said.

"Died in a good cause," Frank said. "Worse things to say about a man."

No one said anything for a moment.

"What do you say, brothers?" Jesse asked.

"I'm in." Clell Miller took out two more melons.

Bob Younger fanned his pistol. "Them banks better watch out for me."

"I ain't never ducked nothin'." Ed Miller exploded four more melons with his rifle, and a little cheer went up from the kids.

"Just come this way once," Jim Younger said. "Might as well have some lively times." He fired at the wagon.

"What about you, Frank?" Cole asked.

Frank grinned at his old friend. "I'm ready to charge." Jesse looked across at Cole. "You in?"

Cole aimed his Winchester at the wagon. "I always thought I was the fella that had the idea." He fired.

"Looks like y'all had a lot of fun!"

The gang turned to see the six-foot-six-inch frame of Silas Dunham standing in front of his livery stable. None of them said a thing.

"Well, that's mighty fine," Dunham said. "But them melons belonged to me."

"That's a shame," Jesse said.

"Goddam right it is!" Silas Dunham held up some harness in his right hand. "Now someone's gonna give me some cash money for them melons, or I'm gonna whip it out of him." Dunham advanced a few steps. "Them guns of yours don't scare me at all."

"Man's right." Jesse knew that Dunham was not joking. "Pay him, Frank."

Frank peeled off a bill and handed it to Dunham. "Five dollars enough?"

"Reckon it'll do."

Bob Younger smiled at Mr. Dunham. "Them's gonna be some famous melons someday."

Dunham shook his head, turned, and walked back into the livery stable.

"Melons, huh?" Jacob Rixley shook his head at Frank's tale. "Doesn't sound like any noble cause to me. What happened next? You just up and robbed the bank?"

"Had to get our uniforms first," Frank said. " 'Course, that was Jesse's idea too. I told you, he was the one with all the fancy plans. I guess he always thought it was our right to be out there robbin' banks and all. He almost told the world before we started."

'What?" Rixley asked.

"Really. We went to this hardware store, Huddleston's I believe it was, to get our dusters and our other gear. I was standing right by Jesse while he was loading his gun. He says to Mr. Huddleston, 'Damn railroads comin' through hurt a lot of folks.' 'What can you do?' Huddleston says. Jesse was aimin' to tell him, too, until I put my hand on his shoulder. I said, 'We're workin' on it, Mr. Huddleston.' "

"The old boy probably wouldn't've minded," Rixley said.

Frank shrugged. "Maybe not. Anyway, as we were leaving, Jesse leans over to Huddleston and says, 'Damn banks make it hard for a man to keep his land. We aim to do something about it.' Huddleston nodded at him, lookin' real sad. 'Times've changed when you can't hold your head up in your own state.' Then Jesse gave Huddleston one of those long looks of his, like he knew what Huddleston was feeling. 'You in the war?' Jesse asked him. Huddleston looked at Jesse for a minute. Then he said, 'If I wasn't, I don't know where my leg went.' "

"So I guess you were like a little army," Rixley said.

"Only one it was important to was Jesse."

"I doubt it," Rixley said.

"How would you know?" Frank asked.

"Oh, come on, Frank. A uniform pumps a man up."

"Maybe so. But when we come out of Huddleston's, the only one pumped up was Jesse. He took me off to the side and actually stood at attention in front of me."

"Too bad Quantrill didn't have uniforms," Rixley said. "Might've saved us from all this."

"Wait a minute," Frank said. "Jesse actually stood in front of me and said, 'Do I look all right?' Now, I thought we all looked pretty silly, to tell you the truth, but all I said was, 'Sure thing.' Then I started to walk away. He grabbed my arm and pulled me back. 'Really, Frank?' he asked me. 'Fine,' I said. 'It's gotta be right,' he said, real strong. 'I gotta look right when I go back into action again.' "

"Don't tell me the rest of you boys didn't catch the spirit," Rixley said.

Frank shrugged. "It was off and on with me, especially while we were robbin' banks and stages. Tell you the truth, banks always scared me, and after Northfield I know why. But there were times, though. Yeah, you're right. First time we rode down to take a train, all in them dusters, we were lookin' mighty fine."

3

What Frank thought of as the first time was really the
first successful time, the time when the James/Younger
Gang (or the Younger/James Gang if you were talking
to Cole) pulled off a robbery of the Rock Island and
Pacific Railroad that went like clockwork. Like anything
else, robbery took practice to perfect, and there had been
a few occasions when the famous outlaw band looked
about as professional as a bunch of school kids.

The gang had made a small reputation from a few bank
and stage robberies, and most of the boys would have
been content to continue in those pursuits. But Jesse James
was always looking to expand, as though he were the
president of a growing business or the manager of a
family store. He probably would have made a good execu-
tive for the banks or the railroads. At first he thought it
would be best to use the cover of the woods to rob a
train. He and the gang waited behind a tree line while
Cole went down and threw a switch that was supposed to
send the train down a short line, where its payroll would
fall into the hands of seven handsome Missouri boys. Cole
threw the lever, scrambled back up the hill, mounted his
horse, and pulled on his black mask. The train hit the
junction a few minutes later. Jesse had his arm held up,
ready to send his men on their mission. At the crucial instant when they were supposed to charge, the train veered
to the left, staying on the track that went through open
country. Frank took off his hat and smacked Cole on

the shoulder. Jesse just shook his head. "I'll be go to shit," Cole said.

The next time Frank himself got the detail. There was a train that stopped for water a little east of Independence, and once it got going again Frank was to ride after it, climb aboard, run along the top until he got to the engine, then pull out his revolver and order the engineer to stop the train. The gang would be waiting, and they'd do the rest. The train passed the abandoned shed where Frank was waiting, and he let the caboose get pretty far past him before he commenced his chase. The train was still going slow, so he didn't reckon on much trouble. By the time he finally got next to the tracks and spurred his horse into a gallop, the train was going nearly as fast as he was. Frank raked the mare's sides with his spurs, and at one point closed the gap between himself and the caboose to about six feet. He stretched out his arm toward the rusty metal railing and rode hard for two or three minutes. By then he was thirty yards behind, the distance widening every second.

When Frank caught up with the gang, Bob Younger was the only one laughing. Bob hadn't fought with Quantrill, and he was always anxious to prove his courage. He was also a superb horseman for his age. Since Jesse's method hadn't been proved unsound—only Frank's execution of it—Bob volunteered to chase the next train. He said, "Besides, Frank's poetic nature makes him more fit to be takin' the diamond bracelets from off of rich ladies' wrists." If Frank had not been so tired, he would have whipped the wise-ass Bob.

The next spot they picked was outside of Sedalia, and Bob Younger rode his mount right up to the caboose and jumped on the platform as though he were a paying customer. He climbed the ladder to the roof, then ran down the catwalk toward the locomotive, leaping from carriage roof to carriage roof. He only fell once before he saw the bridge. At first he just figured on lying down and going under it with the train. Once on his belly he looked up and saw that the bridge was low enough to divide him lengthwise if he stayed where he was. He didn't even have time to get down one of the ladders between the cars, so he rolled to the left and ended up watching the caboose go by from a muddy ditch at the side of the track. Frank didn't laugh at him, but Bob hurt so bad that he got a bottle of whiskey and stayed in bed for three days.

"Our problem," Jesse said, "is gettin' the train stopped."

"Shee-it!" Cole spat tobacco juice into the bucket between his feet. "Our problem is we're broke."

"We gotta plan carefully," Jesse said.

Cole gave Jesse a look. He never did like it when Jesse acted like a general. "Plans ain't puttin' nothin' in our pockets. I say let's all board the goddam train, and if Bob here can't get it stopped, we'll jump off with our pockets full of loot."

Jesse nodded slowly. "You might have something. I've got to think it over."

"Think it over in the saddle," Cole said. "I think we should ride."

They headed for Kansas, and four days later Frank and Jesse James and Cole, Jim, and Bob Younger sat on their horses at the top of a rise watching the Rock Island and Pacific train chuff across the endless prairie. The sky was a perfect blue with a few puffs of white clouds away to the south. The men all wore gray cattle dusters with black collars, and if it weren't for them all wearing different styles of hats, they would have looked like a team of riflemen in uniform.

Cole grinned at the sight of the train. He jacked a round into his Winchester, then nodded at Bob. "Go get 'em, baby brother. I don't reckon there's a bridge for a state and a half."

Bob let out with a rebel yell and spurred his horse toward the train. In a moment Frank and Jesse followed him. Cole looked at Jim. "Brother, it looks like we're about to expand our occupational horizons."

"Let's do it then," Jim said. "There's some new fillies back in Independence that I'd like to see." The two older Youngers galloped down the hill.

The train wasn't going too fast, so when Bob Younger's horse drew even with the caboose, Bob looked over his shoulder and flashed a grin at Frank James. Frank just shook his head as Bob vaulted onto the platform, but he laughed aloud when Bob tucked his thumbs beneath the lapels of his duster and stared out at the Kansas landscape as though he were a politician gazing upon a sea of voters' faces.

Frank turned to Jesse, but his brother's face was frozen with a cold determination. Jesse pointed to the other side of the tracks. Frank pressed the reins against the right side of his horse's neck. The galloping mare hesitated for a moment, then vaulted the tracks in one long fluid movement, and Frank felt a sudden exhilaration as he raced for the door of the Pullman car.

In a moment he was there, pulling alongside as Bob Younger leaped from one car to another above him. Jesse's mount pulled even on the other side of the train, and Jesse pointed to the Pullman door and nodded. Frank took his feet out of the stirrups, grasped the platform railing, and slowly slid from his horse and pulled himself up on the car's steps. As he stood at the rear of the car waiting for Jesse to appear at the front, he fingered the butt of his pistol and thought that the sight of people riding in a train was a pleasant one to behold.

Frank looked to the side as the train went by Jesse's riderless horse, then his little brother walked through the door at the front of the car with a six-gun in each hand. Frank drew his revolver and stepped through the back door. The passengers gasped at the sight of Jesse and his guns. "Just stay quiet, everybody," Jesse said, and gave the crowd a reassuring smile. "Me and my brother just want you to sit back and enjoy the journey."

"That's right," Frank said. A man turned and gave him a sour look, and an older woman blushed when Frank winked at her. "We're going to watch over you folks while our good friends borrow the Rock Island payroll."

Outside, Bob Younger reached the end of the catwalk of the last passenger car and looked down at the locomotive, where the engineer and fireman sat talking. He drew his gun and dropped into the tender, letting out a squeal of pain at the sliver that had found its way into his calf. The two men in the engine turned to look at him as he began crawling over the wood, and he pointed his gun at them. Both men put their hands into the air.

"Don't shoot, mister," the fireman said.

"I won't," Bob said, "if you stop this train."

"What're you aimin' to do?" the engineer asked.

"I ain't aimin' to do nothin'. I'm doin' it."

The engineer squinted at Bob's face. "You that bank robber? You Jesse James?"

The question flattered Bob, but he hid his proud feelings beneath a laugh. "Shit no," he said. "I'm Bob Younger. In case you boys hadn't heard, Jesse James rides with the Youngers." He scowled and waved his pistol. "Now how about stoppin' this train?"

"Anything you say." The engineer moved for the brake.

The train began to slow just as Cole Younger slid the crossbar off the mailcoach door. Cole backed off a little and leveled his Winchester as the door swung free. The two Pinkerton men held playing cards in their hands, and the detectives stared in amazement as Jim Younger swung from his horse into the car. Then the fat one with a drinker's nose went for his Peacemaker, but Jim slammed the butt of his Winchester against the side of the detective's head, and the man crumpled in a heap on the floor. Jim smiled at the other Pinkerton. "What your friend just did was real stupid." The other nodded, raising his hands as Cole clambered into the car with his saddlebags over his shoulder.

"Now, would you look at that." Cole gazed lovingly at the strongbox, then raised his rifle and fired five quick rounds into the lock, reducing it to a few shards of metal on the floor. He pulled a grain sack from his saddlebags, kicked open the strongbox, and fell to his knees in front of it. "Well, Jimmy, it looks like you'll be able to commit the sin of fornication more than once." Cole guffawed and stuffed the stacks of bills into his bag.

"And you'll be able to play poker for at least half an hour," Jim said.

"If I bet real careful," Cole said. He slammed the lid back down on the empty box and slid the grain sack into his saddlebags. "Much obliged to ya," he said to the quaking Pinkerton man. "If you've been following the drift of the conversation you'll know that this money is going to be well spent." He walked to the door and looked toward the front of the slowing train. In the distance he could see Ed and Clell Miller on their horses, holding the reins to five fresh mounts. "I'll be damned," he said. "We really did it."

"You doubted we would?" Jim asked.

Cole snorted. "I doubt everything until it happens." The train came to a halt, and Cole relieved the Pinkertons of their guns and hurled them out onto the ground. "You boys can retrieve those after we're good and gone. If you go after 'em while I can see you it might well be the last move you make." He nodded to Jim. "Let's ride."

They jumped out of the car and ran to where Ed and Clell held the horses. The Miller boys kept their guns on the train as Cole and Jim mounted up. Cole fired his pistol into the air and Bob came running from the engine. Jesse and Frank stepped off the Pullman car and walked leisurely to the horses. "How'd it go, Cole?" Jesse asked.

Cole shrugged. "Like Sioux City on Saturday night."

The James brothers got on their horses, and the seven gang members sat staring at the train for a moment.

"What the hell we waitin' for?" Bob asked.

"Some things deserve lookin' at for a little bit," Frank said.

"You're truly poetic, Frank," Cole said. "But I reckon we've waited long enough."

"Let's ride!" Jesse bellowed. They wheeled their horses around, and the gang headed east at full gallop, firing a few parting shots into the air.

4

Jesse James was not partial to liquor, whores, or gambling, but, like a good general, he knew these things were necessary to keep his men in line. He usually went with them, especially to the better bordellos, where the atmosphere was leisurely and a man could sit back and measure his accomplishments and dream about the future. Olivia Twiss ran such a place in Independence, Missouri, and two nights after their first train robbery the James/Younger Gang took their ease and pleasure beneath her roof.

Jesse sat alone at a card table in the main parlor, smoking a thin cheroot and playing a halfhearted game of solitaire. He kept a glass of whiskey on the table, but would sip from it only three or four times before the night was done. Even indoors he wore his large black hat with the high peak, although it was tipped back on his head, and he wore his black tie loosely knotted. He had cleaned and oiled his guns, had a bath and shave, and felt ready to move at a moment's notice, although he hoped he wouldn't have to. He wanted to relax and bask in the gang's success, and he wanted the boys to have their fill of pleasure from Miss Twiss' ladies.

"Got everything you need, Jesse?" Dorothea, who'd been with Miss Twiss for years, smiled down at Jesse James.

He nodded toward the string band playing a waltz from the corner of the room. "Everything's fine, Dorothea. Just fine."

23

"Be seein' ya." She disappeared into another room.

Even when he smiled there was something unapproachable about Jesse James. He had small eyes that looked both hard and suspicious, eyes that told you that a man's wrong word could be his last. His features were sharp: high, jutting cheekbones, a straight jawline, and a square chin. His nose ended in a point, and beneath it his lips were thin, lips of a man not given to frivolous pleasures. When he rode, the brim of his hat was canted over his forehead, giving him a look all the more impenetrable. In the early days he'd even wondered about himself and what he was about, but lately he'd come to believe in himself as a leader, and he'd accepted the loneliness of command.

It was easy to accept because he didn't really feel it, at least not very often. He loved being on his own to dream up missions, and even when he and the gang went about their business, Jesse's leadership position separated him from the rest. His goals were also different. He wouldn't even confess to his brother that he cared little for the loot they took. Dividing the spoils was the least heroic part of any mission, somehow tarnishing the glory of the act itself. But he didn't let the money part of things get him down. A man had to make a living, after all.

"Wake up, there, little brother." Frank rapped his knuckles on the table, bringing Jesse back from his reverie.

"Hey, Frank." Jesse pulled on his cigar. "How was she?"

Frank shook his head and sat down next to his brother. "I'm gettin' to the point where it's hard to say yes."

"You never had much trouble with that before."

"I ain't like Cole," Frank said. "He likes 'em rough enough to strike a match on."

Jesse smiled. "I thought you did too."

"Times change, and so do people. I believe I'm growing gentle in my old age."

"Don't let it affect your work."

Frank took a sip of Jesse's whiskey. "You'll keep me in line. You always did like givin' orders. Folks are listenin' now."

"I'm just a soldier, Frank."

"That a fact? What makes a good soldier?"

Jesse put his arm around his older brother. "One thing I noticed. It helps if they're family."

Frank guffawed and drained Jesse's glass.

Jim Younger was three days shy of thirteen years old when Freeman Blinn's widow asked him to help her move some furniture, then took him to bed for three hours and sent him home possessed of what he thought was the greatest secret in the world. Unlike many boys his age, Jim was free of any notion that he had been about the devil's handiwork. And a year later, when the widow Blinn became Mrs. Ezekiel Brown and headed west in a Conestoga wagon, Jim Younger exhibited none of the fumbling incompetence of his chums when he began taking girls for extended "walks" in the woods. The widow Blinn had schooled him well, and Jim soon had a reputation that brought him a seemingly endless supply of female bodies. Jim dearly loved the female body, but he'd yet to find one he could love for more than two or three hours at a stretch.

Jim wore the smallest hat of any of the gang members, a black felt job with a small brim and a satin band. The hat naturally came square at the top, but Jim wore it with a groove down the middle, and whether the hat was tipped over his brow or set on the back of his head, Jim always looked like what he was—a sport and a ladies' man. He could look tough and act the same when he had to, but beneath even his meanest look you could see the little boy in him. Cole always said he brought out the mother in those women who took him up to bed.

Olivia Twiss' bordello was a favorite of Jim's. He could always count on the regulars like Evangeline and Wilhelmina, who were still in their prime and knew how to treat a man. Sometimes he got to hankering for an older woman—he supposed it was the memory of the widow Blinn—and Dorothea or Olivia herself weren't bad company for an hour or so. Olivia was a shrewd businesswoman, and you could always count on her to have two or three new girls that would keep the townsmen coming back, if only out of curiosity. Jim spied one as he came down the stairs after having his bath, a tall strawberry blonde who was probably still in her teens. He gave her his best smile.

"How do you do?"

"I do fine," she said.

"Mind tellin' me what name you go by?"

"Folks call me Eliza May." She smiled, and Jim noticed a black tooth partway back in her mouth.

He touched her arm. "Well, Eliza May, I may just be sayin' 'May I' a little later this evening."

"What's wrong with right now?"

"Now that's the sort of thing I like to hear. You know, I've seen a lotta gals in your line of work—"

"Braggin'?"

Jim put his arm around her. "Now you just let me finish. I was gonna say that I never seen one quite as pretty as you."

"Is that a fact?"

"That surely is."

"I know I'm pretty," Eliza May said. "I think I could make more money in St. Louis. Maybe even New Orleans."

Jim shook his head. "You stay around here and you'll make plenty of money. You'll also get to see me more often."

"I guess that's supposed to be quite a thrill."

"You'll be my special gal whenever I'm in town."

"Won't lower the price none."

"Awwww!" Jim flicked his hand through the air. "Why don't we go upstairs and talk about that."

As Jim and Eliza May stepped briskly up the carpeted stairs, the band picked up its tempo. The guitarist stood up and sang.

"Oh, we'll rally round the flag, boys
We'll rally once again,
Shouting the battle cry of freedom;
We will rally from the hillside,
We'll gather from the plain,
Shouting the battle cry of freedom . . ."

In the anteroom next to the parlor, Clell Miller and Cole and Bob Younger sat playing poker with two townsmen. Cole, wearing four days' worth of stubble and the dust and sweat from the trail, studied his cards and looked up. "You boys hear what I do?"

Bob Younger sat behind a small mountain of poker chips. "I hear it."

Clell Miller threw down his cards. "I'm out." He nodded toward the parlor. "I think I better talk to that fella."

As Clell got up, Cole eyed the townsman across the table, then looked at his dwindling stack of chips. "I'll see ya the twenty and raise the same." He shoved two blue chips into the pot.

The guitarist did a double take when he saw Clell lumbering toward him. Clell was the biggest member of the James Gang, and the farmer's overalls and thick-soled boots that he wore even to the whorehouse made him look all the bigger. He had fleshy cheeks and twinkling eyes, and even when he was feeling mean, you might think he was about to burst out laughing. If you didn't know him.

Clell walked right up to the guitarist, put his hand on his shoulder, and looked him up and down. The man quit playing, and so did the rest of the ensemble.

"What can I do for you, mister?" the guitarist said to Clell.

"You got nice hands," Clell said. "Real purty."

The guitarist smiled nervously.

"Wanna keep 'em?" said Clell.

The smile faded, and the guitarist nodded tentatively. "I'm sorry about the song. It was just a request. Nothing personal."

"Well," Clell said, "I got a request of my own. 'I'm a Good Old Rebel.'" Clell fished a coin from his pocket and dropped it in the band's box. The guitarist nodded his thanks, and the group quickly fulfilled the request.

"Good goin', Clell," Jesse said from across the room.

Clell shrugged and grinned. In truth he didn't care much for the song, but was happy if it gave the boys a thrill. "Hold it, Wilhelmina," he said to the prostitute as she started around him.

"Sorry, Clell. I got a customer waitin'."

"Just wanted to know if you'd seen my brother."

"Round back with Evangeline, I reckon. Think he's got a load on."

Clell patted Wilhelmina's rear as she walked away, then went out in back to wait for his brother.

The townsman spread his straight on the table and raked in the pot. As Cole dealt the next hand, Bob looked around him to watch the fight that had suddenly broken out in the parlor. One of the combatants pulled out his pistol and knocked his adversary cold with the butt. Two of Olivia Twiss' finest whores knelt to aid the unconscious man. Bob Younger took two cards.

"What the hell was that all about, Cole?"

"I wouldn't know." Cole took four cards.

"I wonder who the hell that fella was," Bob said.

"Since I didn't even turn around, I wouldn't know." Cole tried not to smile at his three aces, and he only raised twice as the bidding went around.

"Say, Cole," Bob said, "you remember Clyde White-head?"

Cole didn't, and he shook his head.

"I hear he's been askin' for ya. He says you killed his cousin. They was both Union men."

One of the townsmen saw Cole's bid and raised him again.

"What'd his cousin look like?" Cole asked.

"Like a piece of rope with a knot in the end."

"Guess I'll have to take Clyde's word for it." Cole looked at the townsman. "I call."

The townsman only had three jacks, and Cole greedily reached for the pot.

"Hold it, brother," Bob said. "Crowded cabin'll beat them aces." Bob rolled three tens and two treys.

"Ain't fair," Cole said. "I reckon we'll have to rob a bank tomorrow."

If you saw them side by side, you wouldn't have known that Ed Miller was even related to Clell, let alone his brother. You would be more apt to mistake him for Jim Younger's brother (although Ed's prettiness was marred by a confused and angry look), or even Jesse James' (although Jesse didn't have that boyish quality that was still a part of Ed). Ed's hat brim was as thin as Jim's, but the hat itself was a real derby with a little V punched right where the top met the sides. Ed liked to drink a lot, and he was always nervous.

He'd received what he'd paid for from Evangeline and was heading down the Twiss back stairs for a strong drink, because the pleasures of the flesh never thrilled him all that much.

"Ed?" Evangeline said.

"What?" He said it as if she'd asked him for a hundred dollars.

"You reckon I could lure old Jesse up to bed? A lot of us would like to know what he's like."

Ed grabbed her arm and scowled. "I don't want to hear nothin' about no Jesse James, you hear? Now get on away from me for a while." He gave Evangeline a little shove that nearly sent her falling down the stairs. Clell appeared at the bottom just as she stepped off toward the parlor. He watched her go, then looked up at Ed.

"She treat you all right?"

"She ain't important, Clell." Ed stopped and sat down three steps from the floor. "You got to smarten up and figure out what's what."

Clell leaned against the banister and gave Ed a puzzled look. "What in tarnation you goin' on about now?"

"About who we ride with, that's what. James and Younger, Younger and James, that's all ya hear anymore. Well, I reckon the Miller boys could go off on their own and split up things two ways instead of seven." Ed wiped his dripping nose on his sleeve. "Wouldn't have to hold no horses, neither."

"Now just go easy, Ed. There ain't nothin' wrong with things the way they are. A couple more robberies and them boys'll give us some room. They're probably a little skitterish of you because you're young."

Ed narrowed his eyes until his brows came together above his nose. "I ain't no greener than Bob Younger."

"I know it." Clell put his hand on his brother's shoulder. "Why don't you go on and have another drink, Ed? Just have yourself a good time and don't worry things too much, hear?"

"I hear ya," Ed said. "I'm gonna go get paralyzed is what I'm gonna do."

"Shit!" Cole said as the townsman raked in yet another pot. "I reckon I'm good for one more." He fingered his few remaining chips. "Deal again."

Belle Shirley wasn't Olivia Twiss' prettiest hooker, but she charged a lot and got away with it because she seldom had an unsatisfied customer. Short and dark with a thin fighter's lip, she carried herself in a way you couldn't ignore. She strode into the anteroom, tucking a handkerchief into her sleeve, and stood behind Cole Younger. She observed his meager stack of chips and shook her head. "You keep losin' at this rate, Coleman Younger, and you're gonna have to go out and rob yourself another train. Scare some more innocent folk half to death."

Cole turned around and half smiled. "Never did like people standin' behind me."

"You ought to be flattered." Belle winked at the townsman. "Ain't often Belle Shirley stands behind a man."

Cole snorted. "Oh, I expect you're right about that." He turned and looked at her again. "Still askin' fifteen?"

"I'm thinking about raising it."

"Ain't nothin' worth gettin' at that price." Cole stared at the table and shuffled the cards.

"So far I don't figure I missed a whole lot," Belle said. "But I'll tell you what I'll do. Twelve and a half for you, since you're about to go broke."

Cole set the deck on the table. "I'll cut you for it. I win, it's free. You win, it's twenty-five."

Belle pointed to the deck. "Make your move, Mr. Big Spender."

Cole picked up half the deck and showed Belle the jack of diamonds and a confident grin.

She gave him back his grin and turned over the ace of hearts.

"I *will* be go to shit," Cole said.

"If your luck changes, feel free to call on me. If those Pinkerton boys don't get you in the calaboose first." Belle turned and walked away.

The string band was playing a slow and sentimental

number, and Jesse James leaned his head back and closed his eyes, realizing for the first time how tired he was. Then someone touched his arm and his eyes came open suddenly.

"Hey, Jesse." Bob Younger, half drunk, flashed a bucktoothed grin and slid into a chair.

"Havin' a good time, Bob?"

"Sure am, Jesse." He nodded toward two girls sitting across the parlor. "These gals around here got the idea that we're somethin' special."

Jesse spread his hands as though there was no doubting it. "I'd say it *was* something special to be the first at robbin' trains."

"Wasn't the Reno brothers first?"

Jesse shrugged. "But they was caught. We're free. And you did a damn good job yourself, Bob."

"You really think so?"

"Sure do."

Bob was very pleased with himself. "Makes you want to go after some of these whores, doesn't it?"

Jesse shook his head. "Ain't my way, Bob. I got Zee Mimms waitin' for me."

"Let me buy you a drink, then."

"I don't much like the stuff, Bob. Clouds the thinking, you know what I mean?"

"Makes my head just right." Bob stared at his boss for a moment. "Damn, Jesse, it's a good thing you're an outlaw. Otherwise you'd be dull as potatoes."

"Suppose I would be." Jesse let go with a little laugh.

Evelyn Suggins, a new whore from Bellbrook, Ohio, laid her head on Frank James' shoulder and gently stroked his hairy chest. "Are you really Frank James?" she asked.

"I believe I am." Frank gazed at the ceiling. "Although I suppose I could be a poor dirt farmer dreamin' that I was Frank James. Dreamin' I had money and clean fingernails and a pretty woman by my side." And, Frank thought, dreaming I had robbed a train. Frank had not felt so excited about a robbery in two or three years. He had been afraid before, afraid that the gang was getting in over its head, but his fear had vanished beneath the euphoria of accomplishment. He felt proud of his brother's inspiration, and thrilled by his own derring-do. He felt like a young man again, and he wished that Evelyn was someone for whom he cared more deeply so that he could share his secrets with her without the fear of her laughter.

"Are you married?" she asked.

"No, ma'am." Frank chuckled. "Does that make a difference?"

"I was just curious," Evelyn said. "You know?"

"Sure do."

"How come you picked me?"

"You know how it is." Frank couldn't decide what had been the motivating force. "One thing leads to another. You were willin' and here we are."

"Ain't that the truth." Evelyn raised her head and blew out the candle on the night table. "I reckon we got something to take care of." She suddenly rolled on top of Frank and kissed his neck.

"Easy, Evelyn!" Frank needed a moment to adjust to her sudden passion. "Easy."

Clell Miller was generally partial to Wilhelmina, but since she had the curse that night he ended up with Kate, a strapping young farm girl who was getting ready to move on to California. "You ought to go there yourself," she said to Clell after they'd come down from upstairs and were sitting in the parlor with drinks. "Make yourself some good money."

"I make good money now," Clell said.

"You steal good money now. In California you could probably make the same, legitimate-like."

"Never thought about that." Clell took a drink.

"I reckon. How come you do all this robbin' and shootin' and all?"

"I don't know," Clell said. "Most of us was in the war, and we robbed our first Yankee bank 'cause we didn't know no better and it seemed like a good idea at the time. After that, it seems we was just in the habit. Now I reckon we'll keep going till they lock us up or hang us, one."

"You might even get shot yourself," Kate said.

"Might at that." Clell figured it was inevitable. "Never can tell. Still beats dyin' with a hoe in my hand."

"There's other ways to make a livin' besides farmin' and robbin', you know."

Clell Miller finished his glass of whiskey. "None that I'm fit for, I believe."

5

The James/Younger Gang was so pleased about robbing the Rock Island and Pacific that by the time the men finished celebrating, most of them were broke and needing to go on another job. Jesse James still had most of his money, but he was always ready to lead his men into action, and this time he chose the Gallatin Bank. Jesse rode into town from the west end, Ed Miller at his side. Ed had been a little itchy lately, and Jesse figured to let him in the bank this time, hoping it would make him feel more important. They stopped their horses and tied them to the hitching rail just as Frank and Clell rode in from the east end of town. Jesse and Ed walked into the bank, and Frank and Clell tied up in front of the barbershop.

The entrance faced three tellers' cages, and as Jesse stood by a table and drew a picture of one of the lady customers, the Miller brothers flanked the line of cages. Jesse turned, and Frank nodded to him from the doorway. Jesse crumpled his drawing and threw it in a wastebasket, then strode to the cages, vaulted over, and stood where the money was, holding a pistol to the middle teller's head. "Everyone put your hands up and stay calm. We're just gonna make a little withdrawal."

Outside, Cole Younger fired his shotgun into the air. Bob cut loose with a rebel yell and squeezed off three rounds from his revolver, while Jim galloped after a fleeing wagon and shot twice into the air. Cole wheeled his horse while putting another shell in his gun. The good

34

people of Gallatin were in a mad rush to find places to hide.

An old man in an undershirt leaned out of a second-story window and stared in amazement at the Younger brothers. "What in the hell are y'all doin' down there?" he shouted.

"We're robbin' the goddam bank!" Bob Younger fired his pistol and chipped off some brickwork two feet from the old man's head, a head that quickly disappeared back into the building. "What the hell's it look like?" Bob shouted at the fluttering curtain.

Inside, Frank lined the customers against a wall. "Y'all just stay nice and quiet now. We'll be out of your hair in no time."

Jesse held the grain sack by the drawer as the second teller dropped the money in. Jesse looked up from the sack and caught Ed Miller's nervous eye.

"Make him go faster, Jesse," Ed said.

"He's doin' fine, Ed. Never sacrifice accuracy for speed."

Ed looked toward the entrance. "Watch them people there, Frank."

"You tend to your own, Ed."

"Shut up, Ed!" Clell said. "What the hell's wrong with you?"

Ed looked again at the tellers. "What about the safe?"

"There ain't no safe," Jesse said.

The cashier nodded vehemently. "All the money's in that strongbox and in the cash drawers."

"I don't believe you!" Suddenly Ed vaulted the counter and waved his pistol in the teller's face. "You got a safe hidden somewhere. Now you better tell me or I'm gonna splatter your brains all over this damn bank."

"Honest, mister." The teller's voice quavered.

"Get away, Ed!" Jesse shoved Ed back.

"Ed!" Clell yelled. "You gone crazy?"

Frank had turned momentarily to watch the ruckus, and when he turned back he saw a pistol in a customer's hand. Frank smashed his revolver into the man's hand, and the gun roared and spat its bullet into the floor.

"Watch it!" Ed hollered. The teller's hand was in his pocket, and Ed fired three quick rounds into the man's chest. He fell back, dead, a handkerchief appearing in his hand.

The two women customers began to scream, and as Frank tried to quiet them a tall man took out a pistol and shot Jesse in the chest. Frank killed him with two bullets through the neck.

Jesse gripped his chest and screamed, "Miller, you goddam crazy bastard!"

"Come on!" Clell headed for the door. "Let's go!"

Jesse waved Frank away, and the whole gang ran through the door.

Outside, the Youngers covered the door while the Jameses and the Millers mounted up. The printing on the window read "FIRST FEDERAL BANK, GALLATIN, MISSOURI," and when Bob fired his pistol the glass shattered and spilled out onto the walkway. Cole's shotgun blasted again. "Let's ride!" he yelled.

Jesse and Ed were the last to leave, and as Jesse looked over his shoulder he saw Ed's horse stumble and fall. Ed was pitched into the dirt, and his horse rolled over on its back. The rest of the gang was speeding away, so Jesse reined in his mount, wheeled, and went back. Blood dripped off the arm that Jesse extended for Ed, and when the younger Miller grabbed it, Jesse thought his teeth would turn to powder from grimacing against the pain. Still, he didn't utter a sound, and his face remained set like stone as Ed grappled up behind him and the bay mare fled from Gallatin.

The gang rode hard, punishing their horses for fifteen miles until they reached the river. They let the horses drink half their fill, then walk upriver a mile to a little boat landing where they could steal a skiff. Jesse leaned against a tree and stared at the sand while Frank and Jim loaded the boat. Ed and Clell stood watch, but Cole didn't like the tension he could feel all around him, so he took Bob a few yards off from the others and turned around so they could watch downriver. "How long you figure it's gonna take a posse to get here?" Bob asked.

Cole shook his head. "Ain't gonna be one. You know these lazy boys around here, Bob. They'll ride ten miles, get tired, head back, and call the Pinkertons."

That seemed logical to Bob. "Then how come we're standin' guard?"

Cole arched a gob of brown spit onto the water. "Because every once in a while I'm wrong."

Frank finished with the boat, then wet a rag and went over to Jesse. "How ya doin'?"

"I'll live." Jesse scowled, then grimaced with pain as Frank washed his wound.

"Me and Jim'll take you upriver to Mimms' place. We can get the bullet out there."

"You ready, Jesse?" Jim yelled from the boat.

Jesse looked at Jim, then at Ed Miller. "Just about."

Ed Miller dropped his eyes.

"Come here, Ed," Jesse said.

Cole and Bob turned around.

Jesse stood up, and after a moment Ed did too. They began walking toward one another, and when only a yard separated them Jesse lashed out with his right fist and knocked Ed flat.

"Shit!" Jesse yelled, clutching his shoulder in pain.

Ed lay in the sand, rubbing his jaw. "What the hell was that for?"

Jesse stared down at him. "Gettin' panicky and shootin' folks. That guy was tryin' to blow his nose."

Ed stood up, and when he took his hand away from his jaw, Jesse knocked him down again.

"And that's for damn near gettin' me killed."

"Jesse!" Frank yelled.

Ed got up again. "Shit," he said. "I didn't mean no harm."

"Well, you caused plenty," Jesse said. "You're through, Ed. I can't ride with you no more."

Ed stared at Jesse for a moment, then turned to Clell. "You gonna take that offa him?"

Clell had been wondering the same thing himself, but as he looked at Ed's angry little face and Jesse's bloody hand, all his doubts melted away. "I seen what you done in the bank, Ed. It weren't right, and even though you're family, I can't side with ya."

"But . . ." Ed began.

Clell shook his head. "You're on your own." Clell turned his back to his brother and mounted his horse.

Jesse walked over to the skiff, then turned to Cole. "Give Ed his cut, Cole."

Cole nodded and pulled a wad of money from his pocket as Jesse got in the boat and sat down. Frank James grabbed the oars as Jim pushed the small boat out into the river. "See y'all later," Cole said.

"You know the way to Mimms'," Frank yelled.

"Got a little visitin' to do first." Cole turned and edged his horse over by Ed. He shook his head slowly, then dropped a wad of bills that fluttered down around Ed and came to rest on the sand. "You just threw away a real good livin', Ed Miller. Now you listen to me real careful. Any laws get close to us because of somethin' you said, I can guarantee you'll be dead in a week."

Ed scowled up at Cole.

"Think about it," Cole said. "And mind that tongue of yours when you get drunk." Cole turned away and started off with Bob and Clell.

Ed dropped to his knees, scooped up the bills, and stuffed them in his pocket. He looked at the departing horsemen as Clell turned around and gave him a last glance. Ed turned away and watched the skiff moving up-river. To hell with them all, he thought.

6

Clell Miller wore a big brown hat with a wide brim and a gray silk band. The brim went straight out to the edge all the way around; the top of the hat was round, and lately it had begun to remind Cole of the stump of a soldier's leg he'd seen in the war. Bob had exactly the same hat, but he'd bent the brim over his brow a little, and he'd made a nice high peak in the front with the same shape pushed in on either side. Bob's hat made him look a little older than he was, but Cole reckoned that was all right. Clell's hat made him look like more of a plowboy than he already was, or, worse, it made him look like one of those strange religious fellows that hailed from Ohio or Pennsylvania. Not that Cole cared a whole lot about hats. He'd been wearing his own for the last six years. It was a sort of gray with a sort of brown band, but it had so many layers of dirt and sweat and oil and salt that Cole couldn't quite recollect what color it had been originally. He never had liked it until he'd slept under the stars in it a few times.

Cole, Bob, and Clell moved slowly through the woods, following a trail that only Cole knew. No one had said a word for the hour they'd been gone from the boat landing, but then Clell took a pint of whiskey out of his saddlebags and had a long drink. He offered the bottle to Cole.

"Not now, Clell. But you go ahead on. It's a rough thing when your kin goes bad."

"What's done is done," Clell said, handing the bottle to

39

Bob, who did not hesitate to take a belt. "But I don't want to hear nothin' more from nobody about my brother."

"Enough said, then." Cole faced the trail.

"Thanks for the drink," Bob said. "Hey, Cole, where we goin', anyway?"

Cole turned in the saddle and grinned. "Little place y'all know where I owe some *body* twenty-five dollars."

Bob let out a little yell. "I might just have to have me five of them gals."

"Okay with you, Clell?" Cole asked.

Clell nodded and forced a little grin. "I reckon I can live with it."

Belle Shirley lay back in the wooden tub while Levinia, one of Olivia Twiss' maids, poured hot water from a pitcher over her shoulders. "That feels real nice, Levinia," Belle said. "That Kansas boy gave me a bruise last night."

"You ought to take a rest," Levinia said. "You work too hard, Belle, if you don't mind my sayin' so."

Belle laughed. "Hell, I don't mind. But this work's like any other. You gotta work hard to get ahead. I don't plan to be on my back all my life." Belle closed her eyes and listened to the thud of boots come down the hallway. They stopped suddenly, and in a moment Belle's door flew open and there stood the outlaw Coleman Younger.

Belle put on her toughest look. "Most people knock."

"I expect they do." Cole took three steps into the room.

Belle looked up at Levinia and pointed to the door. The maid left meekly, and Cole tipped his hat to her.

"Well," Belle said, "what can I do for you?"

"Decided that maybe it was time to pay you that twenty-five dollars."

"You did, huh?"

"That's right."

"Gallatin Bank must've paid off pretty well."

Cole nodded.

"Just tell me this. How many girls you visited ahead of me?"

"This is my first stop."

She studied Cole for a moment, knowing that he had come as close as he could to asking for anything. She gave him a little smile as she reached back and pulled out the pin that held her hair in a bun. When she stood up, the brown locks cascaded over her shiny wet shoulders. "Well, here I am," she said.

Cole reached his foot back and kicked the door shut.

By the time Clell Miller had finally found his way to Wilhelmina's bed, he was blind drunk. His performance went accordingly, and even though Wilhelmina had a soft spot in her heart for Clell, after thirty minutes of futile humping she bucked him off and went to get a towel. "Sorry, Clell," she said. "But I got to save something for the other customers."

"I am not my brother's keeper," Clell said, and rolled on his stomach and passed out. He lay there wheezing while Wilhelmina and Levinia got the bath ready, and he finally roused himself and stumbled to the tub after an icy cloth had been placed on his rear end and Wilhelmina had slapped his plump cheeks for several minutes.

Before getting in the water he put on his hat and retrieved his bottle of whiskey, and as he drank, the holy spirit quickened within him. He gazed deeply into Wilhelmina's hazel eyes, then raised a finger in the air. He said, " 'I will lead them in paths they have not known; I will make darkness light before them and I will make crooked things straight.' Isaiah 42:16."

"Tell me somethin'," Wilhelmina said. "If you're such a religious fella, how come you're here?"

Clell gazed at his shimmering reflection in the water. "Because, my dear Wilhelmina, life is a mystery."

Kate's mistake, when Bob Younger came barreling into her room, was telling him that she was just getting ready to have her bath.

"Sounds great," Bob said. "I'll take it with ya." He took his hat off, but he got a bigger bottle of whiskey than Clell's pint, and after half an hour Kate began to think that she would soon be growing scales.

They sat at opposite ends of the tub, and after every sip of whiskey, Bob would bring his toes out of the water and splash Kate in the face. "Ha!" he said. "I ain't had this much fun in a long time."

Kate wiped the water off her eyelids. "You sure got strange ideas about havin' fun with a gal."

Bob splashed her again. "You're havin' a good time, ain't ya?"

"I can splash in the tub all by myself." She reached down and stroked his leg. "Come on, Bobby. There's other ways of havin' fun with a gal."

"I suppose you're right about that." Bob took another drink.

"Y'all better hurry up, too. I hear them Pinkerton men are about to get on your tail."

"No worry," Bob said. "I never been known to take a long time."

After Cole Younger and Belle Shirley finished making love, they lay quietly in the bed for twenty minutes. It had been worth it after all, Cole thought, even for twenty-five dollars. Whores were the only women he knew, and he'd pretty much given up on them lately, but he reckoned he'd be visiting Belle again.

"Feel good?" she said.

"Oh yeah. Just fine."

"We get along real well, Cole."

"I won't deny it."

"Maybe you oughta think about makin' an honest woman out of me."

Cole was stroking her hair, and suddenly his hand grabbed a clump, and he pulled her head up and looked her in the eye. "You serious?"

She looked away. "Don't I sound it?"

"Shee-it." He let her head drop on the pillow. "You must be crazy."

After a moment she said, "I just wanted to be respectable for a while. Find out what it feels like."

Cole put his arm around her and stroked her shoulder. "You ain't never gonna be respectable, Belle. You're a whore. You're always gonna be a whore." He pulled her to him and kissed her forehead. "That's why I like ya."

"Well," she said. "Don't worry about it none. I'll probably end up gettin' married lots of times."

7

Jesse James passed out soon after the skiff left the boat
landing, and Frank figured that if it hadn't have been for
his brother's spite against Ed Miller he would not have
made it out of Gallatin. Jesse remained unconscious all
the way to the Mimms farm over the Kansas line, and
after Frank had a good meal and a shave, he took off to
fetch his mother, leaving Jim behind.

Zerelda Mimms—or Zee, as she was called—was a
beautiful woman, but she wasn't Jim Younger's type. Any
woman who could get him shot by Jesse James definitely
wasn't his type, but Zee also had a serious air about her
that Jim didn't care for in a woman. She didn't take to
his jokes, especially if they were about the gang and its
robberies. She seemed to take the business more seriously
than Jesse himself, and Jim reckoned that if she'd been
a man she would've given Jesse a fight for the leadership
of the gang.

Zee's little sister Beth was another matter, and during
the two days he'd been at the farm, Jim had made a point
of teasing her whenever possible. She had red hair and
spunky little blue eyes, and although she tried not to be
impressed with the tales of Jim's exploits, he knew he
made her heart beat faster than any of the sodbusters on
the neighboring farms. But Jim had no designs on Beth;
if something happened in a couple of years, that might
be all right, but he knew Zee would be all over him if he
tried anything now.

Jim stood with Zee out in front of the house, watching

44

the wagon that carried Frank and his ma and his little brother Archie come up the road.

"Yeah," Jim said, "I reckon Cole's visitin' a few old gals he knows. Of course he says it's all for the benefit of Bob's education."

"I thought you'd be the one teachin' him about that," Zee said.

"Ain't got time." Jim looked over and caught Beth's eye. She turned back to the flowers she was picking. "Got to keep my eye on Beth here. Protect her from these locals."

Beth stood up. "I don't need no protectin'."

Jim nodded toward the wagon. "Looks like they made it."

Beth walked over and stood by her sister. "So what are you doin' standin' around with a bottle of whiskey in your hand?"

Jim took a drink. "Restin' up. I believe I might call on that Tebbs girl down the road tonight."

"You mind yourself with Ruth Tebbs," Zee said. "She's young enough to get a grown man in trouble."

Jim winked at Beth. "She's old enough, ain't she, Beth?"

The wagon stopped in front of them.

"Afternoon, Mrs. Samuel," Jim said. "Frank. Hey there, Archie."

"Afternoon," Mrs. Samuel said. She was a large woman with a serious, careworn face. "Where's my Jesse?"

"Jesse's inside restin'," Zee said. "He's gonna be just fine."

"Sure is," Jim said. "Zee's been takin' real good care of him."

Mrs. Samuel gave Zee a mother's look. "How's the nursin', Zee?"

"Patient's mighty stubborn."

"I coulda told you that, sure as you're my namesake."

"Ain't that right," Jim said. "Zee's named after you, isn't she?"

Frank smiled at Zee. "Jesse oughta marry you, Zee. He'd be the only fella I know with a wife and a mother with the same name."

Zerelda Samuel stared at Frank. "You shut your mouth about Jesse gettin' married, Frank James."

Frank got out of the wagon while Jim took another drink.

"And, Jim Younger," Mrs. Samuel said, "I don't mind noticin' that you've acquired a taste for whiskey."

"Helps pass the time," Jim said. He passed the bottle to Frank, who took a drink himself.

Mrs. Samuel shook her head. "Jesse don't drink."

"I'm older," Frank said. "I get thirstier." He turned and faced the wagon. "And Ma, Jesse does drink. He just don't drink around you is all."

Mrs. Samuel ignored her oldest son's remark. "I'm surprised to see you here, Jim Younger. Papers got you and your brothers in Mexico." She smiled down at Zee. " 'Course they got Jesse married to a squaw, too."

"Papers don't get nothin' right," Frank said.

"They print what people like to read," his mother said. "Not many folks I know want the truth."

Frank took another drink. "I ain't part of no fairy tale."

"Cheers folks up to think so," Zee said. "Maybe they got the facts wrong, but they got the spirit right."

Frank was about to retort, but turned toward the house when he heard the front door slam. Jesse stood on the porch without his shirt or hat, a large bandage around his chest.

"Ma," Jesse said. He walked slowly down the stairs as his mother came toward him.

"Hello, son."

" 'Bout time you got out of bed," Frank said.

Jesse and Zerelda Samuel looked at each other as though no one else were there.

"Thought I heard you talkin', Ma," Jesse said.

"How are you, son?"

"Ma." Jesse James embraced his mother. "I'm awful glad to see you, Ma."

8

Charlie Ford wasn't quite six feet tall, and although he was only in his early twenties he was already adding a layer of fat to his belly. That's what comes with old age, he thought. He dumped the bucket of slop over the fence into the muddy pen, then watched for a moment as a sow made for the garbage and began rooting. Charlie turned and hurled the bucket toward the ramshackle house fifty feet away. The clattering stopped, and a woman bellowed from within the house, "Cut out that goddam racket!"

"Shee-it!" Charlie Ford got down on his knees and picked up a little stick. He shoved one end through the fence and rubbed it up and down between the sow's eyes. The porker returned several pleasured grunts. Charlie's brother Bob, just turned twenty, walked over and leaned against a fence post.

"Don't disturb the girl, Charlie. She's workin'."

"Sh!" Charlie whispered. "Can't you see I'm tryin' to hypnotize Amanda here?"

"Sorry, Charlie." Bob gazed off into the distance. Although he was two inches taller than his brother and stronger in the arms and shoulders, he felt that Charlie possessed a superior wisdom, and Bob seldom contradicted him.

Inside, the three-room house was a mess. In the back room, Lucy Ford lay in the lumpy bed while Eldon Runkle, a traveling horse-liniment salesman, panted away on top of her. "Come on, for God's sake," Lucy said.

"I'm just gettin' rolling," Eldon wheezed.

47

"You kiddin'?"

"No, ma'am."

"Jesus." Lucy pushed him to the side, jumped out of bed, and slid on her nightgown.

The confounded Runkle grabbed her by the arm. "I told ya, I'm just gettin' started."

"Now I'll tell you," Lucy said. "You're finished. Pay up and get the hell out."

"I don't pay for what I don't get. Now you get in that damn bed."

"Like hell." Lucy jerked her arm free and ran to the window. "Hey, Bob!" she yelled. "This one ain't payin' me."

"Comin'," Bob replied.

Eldon Runkle managed to get his drawers and his trousers on before Bob Ford got to him. Bob marched him out the front door and threw him off the porch into the mud. Charlie had released Amanda from her trance long enough to get the remainder of Runkle's clothes and his sample kit, and the elder Ford threw these things down on top of the baffled salesman. Lucy stood in the doorway buttoning up her dress while Bob Ford pulled his revolver.

"Don't you think you should handle this, Charlie?" she said.

Charlie shook his head. "Let's see how little brother does."

Bob menaced Runkle with the pistol. "You owe my sister a dollar for the first fifteen minutes."

"And how!" Lucy said. "And fifty cents for each fifteen thereafter."

"That comes to . . ." Bob began counting on his fingers.

"Two dollars," Lucy said.

"I didn't finish, and I ain't gonna pay," Runkle said defiantly.

Bob Ford cocked his pistol. "You mean my sister didn't make you happy?"

"We laughed a lot, but that's about all." Eldon Runkle looked to the side. "Takes me a while."

Bob Ford snorted. "I ain't got that problem, mister. And I got no sympathy for it." At five-second intervals he pumped three rounds into the mud at Runkle's feet, and by the time he finished he had two dollars in his hand.

Eldon Runkle pulled on his boots and made a beeline for his horse.

On the porch, Charlie Ford turned to his sister. "Another satisfied customer, huh? Everything all right?"

"Just what do you think?" Lucy turned and stomped back inside the house.

Charlie walked down the steps and stood next to his brother, watching Runkle flee. "Bob, how much more of this can we take?"

"Question is, Charlie, how much more of this can she take?"

"I'm serious. Listen, why in hell can't we go off and try something different? This ain't exactly the end-all, be-all, you know. At least I hope it ain't."

"What do you mean?" Bob asked. "You gettin' tired of this fancy hotel and all the fine company that comes visitin'?"

Charlie Ford surveyed the house, the barnyard, and his contented sow, then began walking toward the road that Runkle had just taken.

"Where you goin'?" Bob asked.

"To get me some new duds." Charlie Ford gave his little brother a wise and confident look. "I want to look real good when I run into those James and Younger boys. They ain't gonna want to hire somebody that's lookin' all run-down and poorly."

Bob smiled at his brother and shook his head. "You really think we could ride with them boys?"

"Sure do."

"I'll be damned. Well, wait for me, Charlie." Bob Ford caught up with his brother. "How we gonna pay for these duds?"

Charlie pointed to the two dollars in Bob's hand. "Lucy always did say she wasn't in it for the money."

"It ain't gonna be enough," Bob said.

Charlie slapped him on the back. "We'll steal the rest. We're robbers now, and don't you forget it."

9

As Jacob Rixley rode into Independence, Missouri, for the first time, he caught a feeling of disrespect for the law that he hadn't expected. It went deeper than people's natural aversion to lawmen, a feeling that Rixley himself shared at appropriate times. The men he brought with him, Lull, Wicher, Rasmussen, and Timberlake, had all warned him that raising posses to pursue the James/Younger Gang would be no easy matter. For Rixley the gang was nothing but lawbreakers, pure and simple, and he thought all reasonable men would see it the same way. "Sometimes Missouri reason is a little different from Chicago reason," Lull had said. As they rode down the main street, Rixley looked at faces and knew that what Lull had said was true.

Still, he tied his horse up in front of the post office, and while his men stood to the side, he tacked up a wanted poster and turned to face the gathering crowd. "The Pinkerton Company in conjunction with the Union Pacific Railroad is offering one thousand dollars reward for information leading to the arrest of members of the James/Younger Gang."

There was no response from the townsmen. Jacob Rixley stared for a moment at a hard-looking man in front of the crowd. The man shook his head at Rixley. "I ain't got nothin' against the Jameses and the Youngers. They're Missouri boys."

Rixley shrugged and moved down the street with his men.

Charlie Ford, wearing a new dark suit and a large tan hat, stepped up onto the walkway and faced the crowd. "Look at that." He pointed to the poster. "The Jameses and the Youngers are standin' up to the railroads, and this is what they get."

A few members of the crowd mumbled agreement.

"Goddam railroads," Charlie said. "They grab the land, cheat the farmers, and make huge profits. It ain't right."

"That's the truth," a townsman said. "They're the enemy of the honest poor fella, and there ain't no mistake about it."

Charlie Ford was fired by the response. "Railroadmen wait till harvest, then burn crops and force people to sell land cheap. Fellas that run the banks are just as bad. Sons of bitches, every one of 'em. They're the enemy, not Jesse James and his gang."

The crowd applauded Charlie Ford as he stepped down and walked across the street. His brother Bob leaned against a post near the blacksmith's shop, wearing a gray three-piece suit and a black hat.

"That was a good speech, Charlie. Maybe you got the gift for politics in ya."

"No thanks," Charlie said. "Looks like Jesse and them boys are gettin' a lot of attention, don't it, Bob?"

Bob agreed that it looked precisely that way.

"Well, little brother, the Ford boys gonna be right up alongside them pretty soon."

Jacob Rixley's mood darkened as he walked down the street. Near the newspaper office someone grabbed his elbow, and he turned to see a man in a neatly waxed black handlebar mustache who was dressed like a slicker from a Northern city. "Mr. Rixley?"

"That's right."

"My name's Reddick, Carl Reddick. The New York *Herald* sent me out here to cover the story of the James/Younger Gang. People back East are interested in following it."

Rixley smiled. "Might say I'm interested too, Mr. Reddick."

"What do you think your chances are of bringing them in?"

Rixley exhaled sharply and stared at the ground, then he faced Carl Reddick. "That's an awfully dumb question." He stepped off after Lull and Wicher as Reddick laughed softly behind him.

Farther down the street, Rasmussen and Timberlake stood by the entrance to the hardware store, watching the small posse forming in the middle of the block. Clell Miller stepped out of the store with a gunnysack full of provisions over his shoulder. Right away he recognized Rasmussen and Timberlake for laws, but when they looked at him he simply nodded and smiled and walked over to them.

" 'Scuse me," Clell said.

"Yeah?" Rasmussen replied.

Clell nodded in the direction of the posse. "What's goin' on over yonder?" He knew he'd be one of the last people to be taken for a member of the famous outlaw band.

Rasmussen drew himself up seriously. "The Pinkerton Company's startin' to raise a posse to go after the James Gang."

"That a fact?" Clell said. "Don't reckon you're gonna have much luck, though. Tell you the truth, I sort of like them boys. Like the way they take on them railroads."

Timberlake shook his head. "For some reason it's hard to get folks pumped up against the James boys and the Youngers."

"How about the Millers?" Clell asked. "Heard they was pretty mean. Everybody talks about the Jameses and the Youngers, but I heard them Miller boys was pretty dangerous customers." Clell gave the Pinkerton men a wide grin.

"Ain't but one of them," Rasmussen said. "The other one was throwed out of the gang. The Millers is small fish compared to the rest."

Clell's smile faded.

"You with us?" Timberlake asked.

"Naw," Clell said. "I reckon I'm like most folks. Ain't got enough agin' them boys to risk my neck tryin' to find 'em. They awful clannish. Got kin all around. Probably some in this town right now."

"I'm gonna tell you somethin', mister," Timberlake said. "We're gonna get 'em."

"Good luck to ya," Clell said. He started to leave, then turned around. "Which way y'all headin', case I change my mind?"

"Columbia Road," Rasmussen said.

Clell saluted them from the brim of his hat.

10

Jesse James seemed to mend a whole lot faster once he found out that the Pinkertons were organizing against him in Missouri. He took long walks with Zee, spent some time on horseback, and even practiced with his gun. He spent a lot of time thinking and talking with the boys, and since none of them seemed to care much he decided to go on down to Arkansas and rob the Little Rock stage. He planned a long operation, and figured to throw in a few banks on the way, maybe even another train. "I don't know how long we'll be gone," he said to Zee as they walked through a field below the house. They could hear the plaintive duet played from the porch. Clell was on fiddle, Bob Younger twanging the Jew's harp. The summer afternoon was lazy and humid, and it didn't seem like a time to be going anywhere.

"But why do you have to leave tomorrow?" Zee asked. "You've hardly given yourself time to heal."

"Gotta get back to things. Ma needs some money to keep the farm going."

Zee snorted. "I reckon your ma can keep a farm goin'. Few other things to boot."

"And I got plans for my future," Jesse said.

"Is that a fact?"

"Besides, the others ain't no good without me. They get drunk, got no discipline. They gotta have somebody to make the plans. Don't worry, Zee, I'll come back for you."

In the yard, Jim Younger pushed Beth Mimms on a tree swing. He was glad they'd be leaving the next day.

He never could sit still for too long, and he wanted to find out how the gang was going to function without Ed Miller, although he figured it wouldn't mean much more than a larger share of the cash. That was fine with him. Mainly he wanted the action. He was starting to feel too settled sitting around the farm.

"What you doin' pushing me on this old swing?" Beth teased. "You oughta be over at Ruth Tebbs' place."

"I might get down there tonight," Jim said. "She's awful good-lookin', don't you think?"

"If you say so, Jim Younger. 'Course every fella around here has been to visit her."

Jim gave Beth an extra-hard push. "Guess you never have that problem, do you, Beth?"

"I have just as many visitors as I want." Beth looked over her shoulder. "And you can count on it."

"Oh! Who might they be?"

"That's for me to know and you to find out."

"Well, how am I supposed to know if you won't tell me?"

Beth tipped her head back and gave a little giggle. "Jim Younger, there are some things a man does not ask a lady."

When the swing got back to him, Jim grabbed the ropes and stopped it. He turned Beth around. "Well, Beth, when you're old enough to call yourself a lady, I'll try to remember that."

Jesse picked an old dandelion and blew the gray fluff at Zee. "Think maybe we oughta get married? Is that what you want?"

Zee shrugged. "You proposed to me before. 'Course that was a long time ago, during the war and all. Guess you had so much on your mind you forgot about it."

"It didn't mean much then," Jesse said. "Except that I knew you were the one. But I didn't have nothin' worked out back then."

"That's a mouthful, Mr. Jesse James."

Jesse grabbed her arm and stopped her. "What you got to figure out is if you want to get up on the horse with me. I'll be honest about it, Zee. I ain't changin' the way I live."

Zee smiled at him for a moment. "It ain't right to try and change a person." She came in close and put her cheek against Jesse's chest. "Truth is, Jesse, I wouldn't like you any other way."

Cole Younger leaned against a tree up in the yard, watching Zee and Jesse down in the field. Next to the tree Frank James was splitting wood with an ax on a large stump. Cole turned to Frank and shook his head. "Next thing you know they'll get married and settle down."

Frank split a log and looked at Cole, "First part, anyway. He's askin' her today."

"You know it don't go with the way he's livin'."

Frank picked up another log and set it on the stump. "Jesse'll be fine."

"Says you." Cole pulled at the stringy hair that hung down to his shoulders. "First gettin' shot, then gettin' married. Bad habits. Watch it, Frank!" Half of the split log had nearly hit Cole's foot.

"Sorry." Frank took out his handkerchief and wiped his brow. "He's old enough to pick his own habits, Cole."

Jesse and Zee walked up the road toward the house, arm in arm. "I never asked anybody else," Jesse said. "I didn't think about anyone else either, but I had a lot of chances."

"I ain't thought about no one else either," Zee said. "Had some offers, though."

"Oh?"

"One thing I want is a proper wedding."

"I . . ."

"And a white dress."

"I better get back to work," Jesse said. "Sounds like you want the whole county to be there."

"I do." Zee smiled. "A girl only gets married once."

Jesse kissed her. "Unless she marries an outlaw."

She stood back and looked into his eyes. "I'll only get married once, Jesse."

When they kissed, Cole turned away. "I'll see you later, Frank. I'm gonna go soak my head." He walked over to the porch and stood watching Clell and Bob play. The two of them were as lost in their music as Jesse and Zee were in each other. "You fellas play real purdy," Cole said. "Almost brings a tear to my eye." He opened the door and headed for the bottle.

11

Jim Younger booked a seat on the Little Rock stage at Conway, and, wearing a new suit of clothes and carrying a newspaper and a valise, he sat down next to a grizzled Civil War veteran and across from a young couple who looked recently married. They rode for half an hour, Jim reading his paper, the veteran dozing, and the young couple talking quietly to each other. The day was bright and hot, but ten miles outside of Conway the terrain began growing gradually more wooded, and soon the stage was moving under a virtual canopy of leaves. A small breeze came up, and the air cooled perceptibly.

The veteran woke suddenly as the stage went over a bad hole in the road. He looked around at everyone, then took out his pipe and fired it up, contentment slowly spreading across his face. After a while he took the pipe out of his mouth and pointed the bit at the young bride. "Say there, little lady, looks like you're wearin' your Sunday dress for this here trip."

"That's the truth." She smiled pleasantly. "It'll be my first trip to Little Rock. I never been in a town that big before. But Vernon's promised to take me to lots of big cities." She squeezed her husband's arm.

"That's right," Vernon said.

The old vet nodded his head with approval. "How long you two been married?"

"Six months," the woman said.

"I never was the marryin' kind myself," said the vet.

"The kind of life I lead, women spell trouble. Footloose and fancy-free, that's my style." He elbowed Jim Younger. "How about you, mister?"

"Haven't felt the call yet." Jim smiled at the woman. " 'Course if I could meet gals as nice and pretty as this one, I expect I could be persuaded."

Vernon scowled at Jim. "I'll tell you what, mister. You keep watch of your mouth and don't be lookin' at my wife here."

"Sorry," Jim said. "I didn't mean no disrespect."

" 'Course he didn't," the vet said. "He was just bein' polite." He aimed his bit at Vernon. "What's your line of work, anyway?"

"It's none of your business," Vernon said. "But I out-fit miners goin' west."

"Gold minin'! Jesus Christ!" The veteran took a thought-ful puff. "My brother went bust lookin' for gold. Lost his poke in San Francisco and most everything else comin' back across the desert. He always was a fool. Few years older'n me. Died of the grippe three days after Lincoln got elected. I always said it was cause and effect."

"Hey, old man," Vernon said. "Put a cork in it awhile. I want to give my ears a rest."

"Be polite, Vernon," his wife said.

"I'll decide what's polite, Shirley. Now you just hush up too." Vernon leaned toward Jim. "And you give my wife one more look and I'll stop this stage and give you a whippin' you won't forget for a month of Sundays."

"Is that right?" Jim asked.

"You can bet on it."

Jim smiled at Vernon and looked out the window. The stage went past a particularly dense clump of trees and rounded a bend. Fifty yards ahead a tree had been felled across the road. Clell Miller and Frank James stood behind it, their Winchesters pointed at the stage.

The veteran looked out the window as the stage slowed. He grabbed his pipe in amazement. "Goddam! Outlaws! Chickenshit sons of bitches. Get out the guns, boys."

Jim Younger already had his out. With his free hand he reached over and grabbed the veteran's gun, then he tapped the barrel of his own against Vernon's chin. He nodded at Vernon's pistol. "You can just drop that out the window."

The stage stopped.

"Do it, Vernon!"

Vernon complied.

"Well, I'll be goddammed," the veteran said. "You son of a bitch. You're in it with 'em."

As Jim opened the door and backed out, Shirley said, "Do you need to use that kind of language?"

The veteran stared at her in disbelief. "Yes, ma'am, I do. We're bein' robbed."

"Come on out," Jim said.

Jesse James and Cole Younger came out of the woods on their horses. Cole's pistol was pointed at the guard, who still clung tightly to his shotgun. Cole nodded. "I would pitch away that shotgun."

The guard looked around nervously, then threw the gun to the ground.

"Throw down the box, hear?" Jesse said.

The box hit the ground with a thud. Jesse dismounted, destroyed the lock with two shots, then bent to his knees and began filling the grain sack with loot.

Bob Younger came out of the woods, leading his horse with one hand and carrying his pistol in the other. He stopped next to Jim and surveyed the prisoners. "Either of you men fight for the Stars and Bars?"

The veteran perked right up. "Sure did. Proud of it, too."

"I did my part," Vernon said.

Bob took a step forward and extended his hand to the old man. "May I shake your hand? I'm Bob Younger."

The old man grabbed it. "Arthur," he said. "George Arthur."

"Who were you with, George?"

George drew himself up dramatically. "General Jo Shelby. Said I was too old for front-line work, so I quartermastered at Carthage, Wilson's Creek, and Lexington. But I got a few shots in." He waved his pipe at Bob. "You can bet on that."

Bob looked at Vernon. "How about you?"

"Uh, I was with Shelby too."

"Where?" Bob asked.

"Cold Harbor."

Old George Arthur looked at Vernon. "With Shelby at Cold Harbor?"

Vernon nodded.

"Shelby weren't at Cold Harbor," George said. "You're a goddam liar!"

Cole Younger pointed his gun at Vernon. "You want to kill him?"

"I would," George said. "I'd shoot the son of a bitch."

"Ought to," Jesse said, standing up with the grain sack in his hand. "You didn't have to lie about Shelby. If you're a Yankee, be proud of it. Bob?"

"Yeah?"

"I want you to take everything of his, hear?"

"Yeah," Jim said. "Everything."

"Everything," Cole echoed.

"Shit yes," Bob said. He began to reach for Vernon's coat, but George Arthur stepped in front of him.

"Here," George said. "I'll help you." He rifled Vernon's inside pockets, then looked him in the eye. "You're lucky you ain't dead. Son of a bitch."

Jim Younger reached out and took Shirley's arm. "Hope we didn't disturb you too much, ma'am. Didn't mean no harm."

She blushed and gave Jim Younger a weak smile.

"You scum!" Vernon yelled. "You take your hands off my wife."

Jim turned and looked at Vernon. "You wasn't married to this good woman, you'd be dead. Hear that, Vernon? Now you just shut up and maybe I won't put a bullet in ya."

Vernon looked back at George.

"He means it," George said. "And I'll help him."

Jim Younger tipped his hat to Shirley. "I hope you'll forgive me for sayin' so, ma'am, but you coulda done a lot better than Vernon here."

Shirley stared at him as the gang mounted up.

"Be seein' you folks," Jesse said.

The driver spat. "At the end of a rope."

Jesse gave him his best smile. "I don't know how Jesse James is gonna go, but he ain't gonna swing."

Suddenly the gang whirled and galloped away from the stage. Old George Arthur walked after them for a few paces, then stopped and gazed into the distance. "Jesse James. I'll be goddammed and go to hell!"

12

Jesse didn't get around to marrying Zee for a year. After the Little Rock stage, he found it necessary to transact business with a train near Memphis, with the National Bank of Columbia, Kentucky, and with the Planters Bank of St. Genevieve, Mississippi. But when he finally posed for his wedding picture with Zee, Beth, Frank, Archie, and his ma, he felt that he'd accumulated sufficient funds to support a family decently. He didn't think it was right to shirk a thing like that, and he smiled proudly as the powder went off to light the picture. The band began to play, and the others headed out to the dance floor of the Masonic Hall, but Zee clung to Jesse as though she'd never let him go.

Jim Younger stood to the side and watched Beth Mimms come down from the stage. She looked around for a moment, then headed for the back of the hall. Jim stepped in front of her. "How ya been, Beth?"

She stared at him for a moment, looked away, then back again. "Hello, Jim. Heard the news?"

"What's that?"

"I'm engaged to Ed Miller." Beth smiled proudly.

"Ed Miller?"

Beth nodded.

"Oh, Beth, he ain't no good. Besides, you're too young for all that."

"I'm nineteen on the twenty-third of September," Beth said. "I don't want to wait around forever like Zee did."

"But Beth, he's—"

"And I don't want you sayin' nothin' bad about Ed just

'cause Jesse picked on him. Ed told me all about how Jesse got jealous of him 'cause he could ride better."

"We all got our stories." Jim shook his head. "Seems like just a few months ago I was pushin' you on a swing."

Beth shrugged. "While you was pushin', other people was noticin'."

"I noticed you, Beth." Jim Younger didn't know why he was saying all this.

"Fat chance," Beth said. "Your eyes was on that Tebbs girl."

"Come on, Beth. She weren't nothin' serious."

"I hope not, for your sake. She's carryin' Tommy Grattan's baby."

"Ed Miller," Jim said. "He ain't so much. Least Zee ended up with Jesse."

"I told you, don't say nothin' bad about Ed. Truth is, you're just slow off the mark."

"You don't want to rush into things, Beth. You can't undo 'em later."

Beth smiled. "Can't undo this one. Ed's already bought land over past Russelville. 'Sides, we told everybody."

Jim looked away, resolving to let this discussion end. He saw Ed Miller approaching from across the hall. "Ain't much else to say, I guess."

"You could wish me a good life," Beth said.

Jim smiled. "I wish you that."

"Hey, Jim." Ed Miller stood in front of him, grinning. "What ya got to say for yourself?"

"Not a whole lot, Ed."

Ed took hold of Beth's arm. "Well, we want to get some dancin' in. Be seein' ya."

Jim nodded as they walked away. He felt a sudden wave of stupidity engulf him, and for a moment he felt like running out of the hall and getting drunk all by himself. He had never felt like that in all his life. He closed his eyes for a moment, and when he opened them a pretty girl was walking past. She readily accepted Jim Younger's invitation to dance.

Clell Miller had avoided his brother during the wedding ceremony, but when he saw Ed coming across the dance floor he knew they'd have to talk. Clell thought it might not be so bad. People did change—at least a few of them did—maybe Ed had calmed down a little over the past year. Maybe he wasn't so crazy anymore.

Ed stopped a few feet from him, and the two brothers eyed each other for a moment. "How ya been, Ed?" Clell asked.

"I'm fine. How you been, Clell?" Ed's voice still had that nervous edge.

"We're all gettin' on pretty good."

Ed put his arm around Beth. "Beth here's my girl now. We're gonna get married."

Clell nodded. "Heard you two had took up together. Good to see ya, Beth."

Ed smiled again. "I'm real fine, Clell." His face turned cold. "Don't miss you boys none. Come on, Beth." He turned her away from Clell. "Let's get dancin'."

The band moved into a livelier number, and the guests began to clog and buck. Clell Miller was an accomplished clog dancer, but he had no stomach for it now. He watched his brother with Beth Mimms, and it hurt him to realize that he felt more like family with the Jameses and the Youngers than he did with Ed. He tried to ease the pain by telling himself that things didn't always work out in families. That was the way of the world. But when he saw Cole and Frank across the hall and noticed the bottle between them, he thought that might help to ease the pain as well.

When Clell got over to them, Cole was pouring himself a drink and shaking his head. He shook it in Frank's direction. "I believe that Mr. James' brother's gettin' married is interferin' with the function of his brain."

"Shut up, Cole," Frank said. He continued to stare at a young woman who was talking to some ladies by the punch bowl. She wore a gingham dress, and her hair was pinned up neatly in a bun.

"Looks a little too high-class for me," Clell said.

Cole nodded and filled his cup. "If she's too high-class for you, she's too high-class for Frank James."

"I beg your pardon." Frank turned and straightened his tie. "I believe I'm fit for the governor's daughter."

"If they allowed weddings in jail," Cole said.

* * *

Bob and Charlie Ford entered the back of the Masonic Hall and stood there for a moment checking out the crowd. The year had been a lean one for them, but so had all their preceding years, so their complaints were no worse than usual. Each had managed to buy a new shirt, but investment in ties had been deemed excessive.

Charlie spotted Frank, Cole, and Clell, and he gently elbowed his brother. "You scared, Bob?"

"Yeah," Bob said. "Little bit. Expect I am."

Charlie smiled. "We'll just walk up to 'em real steady. We got nothin' to lose."

"That's right," Bob said.

"You let me do the talkin', Bob, got that?"

Bob nodded.

"Do I look all right?" Charlie asked.

Bob brushed a small piece of cheese from the lapel of Charlie's coat. "You look fine, Charlie."

"Let's go, then."

The Ford brothers walked over to the little table and stopped. Both Clell and Cole eyed them for a moment, but Frank was gazing at the lady who had caught his eye.

"You Frank James?" Charlie Ford said, a little too loudly.

Frank's hand went to his pistol as he whirled around. "Who's askin'?"

Cole wiped his mouth with the back of his hand. "Charlie Ford and his little brother, Bob. What the hell you boys doin' here?" said Cole.

"We want to join up," Charlie said. "Ride with you fellas."

Cole poured himself another drink. "Mighty white of you to offer."

"We heard you was lookin' for some new men," Bob Ford said.

"Who'd you hear that from?" Clell asked.

"Your brother," Bob said. "In a saloon a few weeks back."

Charlie Ford put his hand on the butt of his gun. "There ain't a horse we can't ride, a target we can't hit, or a bank we can't rob."

Frank held out his cup, and Cole filled it. "When was the last time you boys went out?"

Bob looked to Charlie for the answer.

"You know how it is, bein' out on the trail and all. We only been out once, but we're willin'."

"What'd you rob?" Clell asked.

"You boys know what it's like," Charlie continued. "It was there and it seemed easy. We just hauled out our guns and made off with it. Down to Joplin it was. They chased us for two days. Y'all know how it is, bein' out on the trail and all."

"What'd you rob, Charlie?" Cole demanded.

"Uh . . ." This time Charlie looked to Bob for an answer, but his younger brother dropped his eyes. Charlie looked back at Cole. "It were a church."

Cole eyed Charlie Ford for a moment, took a drink, and turned to Frank. "What were we talkin' about?"

Frank nodded toward the dance floor. "I was fixin' to ask that lady to dance."

"This I want to see," Clell said.

"Be patient," Frank said. "I'm tryin' to think of the proper words. Maybe a line from Shakespeare or something."

"Snake shit!" Cole Younger said. "I don't know about today. I really don't. Somethin' all wrong about it, and there ain't no way we can start over." He turned his back to the Fords, who had already begun to walk away.

Over by the cake, Jesse James gave Archie a second piece, then stooped down to talk to him. "Archie," he said, "it ain't easy bein' a little half brother." He looked up and winked at his ma. "And now with me gettin' married and Frank off and gone, you're the only one left at home to take care of Ma. You got to take real good care of her, Archie, 'cause that's what she always done for us."

"I will, Jesse," Archie said, gazing reverently at his half brother. "I'll do my best."

"It's only right," Jesse said.

Mrs. Samuel put her hand on Jesse's shoulder. "It's right you should've given that speech a few years ago."

"Oh, I know, Ma," Jesse said. "I just didn't have the words then."

"I reckon you're makin' up for lost time."

"Come on, Ma. Let's dance."

Zerelda Samuel smiled at Jesse James. "Sure thing, son."

Frank James watched his mother and his brother dance, then he looked again at the pretty girl in the gingham dress. "Ain't nothin' for it, boys," he said. "I'll see you later."

Cole took another stiff drink. "I never could see the reason for all this romance."

Frank approached the woman and bowed politely. "Excuse me, ma'am. Would you care to dance?"

She studied his face for a moment, then smiled. "I'd be delighted."

The sound of her voice reminded Frank of honey. "I don't believe I know your name," he said.

"Annie." She curtsied. "Annie Ralston."

"It's a mighty pretty name." Frank took her hand in his.

She nodded. "Why thank you, Mr. Frank James."

Frank let out with a laugh as they danced across the floor.

What Cole wished was that he could get drunk. He'd had enough to take a bath in, but he still felt only a mild buzz. He watched the couples on the floor: Jesse and his ma, Jim and some new gal, Bob and some fat gal, Frank and some new gal. Even Frank, for Christ's sake. Cole thought he had better sense. "It's just you and me, Clell," he said to his last drinking companion.

Clell stared glassy-eyed at the dance floor. "Sort of makes you think about settlin' down, don't it? Find a good woman, give up this outlaw life."

"Oh, Lord." Cole filled Clell's cup and stood up. "I can't drink with you no more, Clell. Can't listen to no more of that kind of talk."

He walked out of the Masonic Hall, only to find a small crowd beginning to gather to bid Jesse and Zee goodbye. Cole moved off to the side with his bottle and was about to sit down on a tree stump when someone yelled, "Hey, Coleman Younger!"

Across the street, in front of the hardware store, Belle Shirley sat in a little buggy. Cole had been avoiding her lately, and he wasn't pleased to see her now.

"Come on over and say hello," she said.

Cole took a drink and walked slowly across the street. "Evenin', ma'am."

Belle nodded toward the Masonic Hall. "Looks like everybody's havin' a real good time at this affair."

"I expect so," Cole said. "Free food and drinks and all."

"How come I didn't get invited?"

Cole looked up at her and smiled. "Because you're a whore." He held her eyes for a moment, then turned and walked back across the street.

"Is that right?" Belle said under her breath. "I suppose it is." Then she bellowed at Cole Younger's back, "At least I ain't a cheap one!" She whipped her horse, and her buggy sped down the street.

Cole did not look back. He stood to the side of the congregation and watched Jesse and Zee shake hands and kiss people as they worked their way through the crowd to their waiting wagon. They could go on their way without Cole Younger's good wishes. Not that he wanted any harm to come to them, but Jesse's having a wife added another complication to the gang's existence, and complications were something Cole could do without. Jesse and Zee waved a final goodbye to the crowd, then drove off into the night. Cole took another drink, straight from the bottle this time.

Frank and Clell stood together at the top of the hall steps, watching the wagon disappear into the darkness. Frank nodded to Annie Ralston as she walked back into the hall, and she smiled at him. His gaze lingered on her for a moment, then he turned to Clell. "Got a question for you, Clell."

"Fire away, Frank." Clell gave him a drunken leer. "Fire away and fall back."

"You ever been in love?"

"Oh, God!" Clell covered his heart as though he'd been

shot. "Yeah. It was terrible. An affliction." He scuffed his boots on the step. "Really miserable. Nothin' but trouble. It drove me crazy."

"That bad," Frank said.

"Yeah." Clell Miller smiled. "She was wonderful."

Beth Mimms and Ed Miller stood near the bottom of the steps. After Jesse and Zee's wagon had gone, Ed turned to his future bride. "Ain't too long and that's us, Beth."

"I reckon." She gave Ed a little kiss. As they started back into the hall she turned to find Jim Younger staring at her, and for a moment she thought she would not be able to look away. Then Ed's grasp tightened on her arm, and she had to turn for fear she would trip on the stairs.

Later that night, when the celebration was just about over, Cole Younger went out behind the Masonic Hall, built a fire, and sat down on a huge log to drink and watch the flames. In a while Jim joined him, and Bob came half an hour later, when the last of the revelers had departed. He twanged his Jew's harp plaintively for a few minutes, then put it away and took another drink.

Jim Younger put his finger in the air and gave his little brother a look of drunken profundity. "Lot of men we used to ride with is dead. Good men. Good cause. Southern gray."

"Good men," Cole affirmed.

Bob looked at both of his brothers. "Goddam good men," he said.

"Here's to 'em." Jim hoisted the bottle. "The memory." He drank.

"We all die," Cole said. "Someday. Everybody dies." He stared at the flames for a few seconds. "One thing's certain, that's death." He reached over and took the bottle from Jim.

"Right," Bob said. "Everybody dies. Right."

The Younger brothers all nodded in agreement for half a minute.

"Hey!" Jim said. "There's a new filly up to Grant's Corner."

Bob grinned. "A new filly?"

Cole pointed at the fire, then jabbed the air with his finger as he spoke. "One thing's certain. That's death."

Bob allowed him a moment of silence. "A new filly?" he asked again.

"Mighty good-lookin'." Jim Younger tipped his head back and looked up at the stars.

"One thing's certain," Cole said.

"I thought you liked Beth," Bob said.

"Aw, hell." Jim rolled off the log onto his back.

"Aw, shit!" Cole picked up the bottle, struggled to his feet, and stumbled away.

13

Jacob Rixley already knew he was up against it, but when he found out that Jesse James had gotten married right under his nose and had sixty guests to boot, he really began to steam. The steam reached a boil a couple of months later when the James/Younger Gang completed their celebration by robbing the Hughes & Company Bank of Richmond, Missouri, and then tying two Pinkerton guards to a stove while they robbed a train outside of Sedalia. Rixley knew that all kinds of folks let Jesse and the gang hide out at their places, and one day he decided he might get lucky if he went straight to the James boys' mother.

He regretted his decision the moment she stepped from the house onto the porch and stared at him, his two deputies, and the eight members of his posse. "Good day," she snapped. "What can I do for you folks?" Archie sat on the railing, not far from his ma.

Rixley took off his hat and introduced himself. "I'm afraid I'm looking for your sons." He pulled a piece of paper from his inside pocket. "I have a warrant here for their arrest."

Zerelda Samuel put her hands on her hips and stared at Jacob Rixley.

"I want your sons, Mrs. Samuel."

"I heard you before," she said.

He waved the paper. "This paper is a warrant from Clay County."

"There wouldn't be any trouble if men like you would

quit hounding my boys." Mrs. Samuel shook her head. "What do you want 'em for?"

"For robbing banks," Rixley said. "And trains."

"Well, you Yankees can turn around and head on back." Mrs. Samuel pointed down the road. "Sounds to me like you got the wrong James family."

"Yes, ma'am," Rixley said, "I am a Yankee, and I am a city man, and I know you don't like either one." He gestured at the men behind him. "But these men with me are Southern and they fought for the Stars and Bars during the struggle."

"Then why are they chasin' my boys?"

"Because they steal, ma'am." Rixley stared at Mrs. Samuel for a moment, then dropped his eyes. "I'm afraid I'm going to have to go in the house and look for them, ma'am. This paper gives me the right to do that."

Mrs. Samuel took a step forward. "You don't set one foot on this porch."

"Come on." Rixley got down from his horse, and Rasmussen followed him up the steps.

Zerelda Samuel glared at them. "Things sure have come to a pretty place when a widow woman with a fifteen-year-old backward baby boy is treated this way and they call it legal!"

"I'm sorry, ma'am." Rixley and Rasmussen entered the house.

Mrs. Samuel turned to the posse. "Damn fools. They ain't in here anyway." None of the posse members looked her in the eye.

By then Rixley knew the James boys weren't in their mother's house, but he didn't know what else to do. A little more pressure might be dangerous, but it might also force the outlaws into making some mistakes.

14

When Jesse James heard that the Pinkertons had been to his mother's house with a Clay County warrant, he called the gang together and they went right down to Liberty and robbed the Clay County Savings Association. Then Jesse headed straight for his ma's. He gave her enough money to keep the farm going for another year, plus he decided to stay around for a while to help her with a few things. His hope was that the Pinkerton man would come back.

Seeing the way Jesse was about his mother made Jim Younger homesick for a family. His folks had been dead for a long time, so he went over to Higginsville and stayed for a while with his Uncle Jack. Jack never had a whole lot to say to the outlaw Youngers. He didn't care that much about what they were doing, but he was worried about his son John. John was only eighteen, worshiped his cousins, and his only desire was to become a long rider with the James/Younger Gang. The second day after Jim had come to visit, John took him for a ride off in the woods. They hadn't been gone for more than fifteen minutes when John said, "How comes I ain't never been asked?"

"I don't know." Jim looked over at him and shrugged. John had a lot of heart, but he wasn't a real big boy. There was something about him—maybe it was the buck teeth—that just didn't look like a fighter. "Maybe you ain't cut out for it," Jim said.

"But . . ."

"Besides, we got plenty of hands the way it is." No one could ever argue with that.

"Well, you keep me in mind, hear? I can rob banks as good as Clell Miller or your brother Bob. Ain't nothin' to it."

"You think so, huh?"

"Shit," John said. "What's to know about robbin' a bank? You ride into town thunderin' like cannon balls, guns blazin', scarin' the Jesus out of every person in sight until they're frozen. Then you ride into the bank without gettin' off your horse, dynamite the safe, and ride off with the loot, hootin' and hollerin' same way as you come in."

Jim began to laugh, then suddenly straightened up in the saddle as he saw two men sitting on horseback by a tree a hundred feet up the trail. "Yeah, right," Jim said. "You seen them two before?"

John Younger shook his head, an angry look spreading across his face.

"Just be cool," Jim said.

They stopped their horses about twenty feet in front of the two men.

"Afternoon." The man who spoke wore a dark-blue suit.

"What's the trouble, friend?" Jim asked.

"No trouble. Just lookin' for the Youngers. You know 'em?"

"Sure I do." John Younger had been carrying his shotgun in the crook of his arm, but he slowly moved it around in front of himself.

"Lots of 'em in these parts," Jim said. "Real big family."

"Who are you fellas?" John snapped.

The other man, who wore a cream-colored suit, said, "Came here to buy cattle."

Jim smiled. "This ain't Texas."

"What about the Youngers?" the man in the blue suit asked.

Suddenly Jim's pistol was pointing at the two men. "You're lookin' at two of 'em," he said. "Now who are you fellas?"

John Younger got off his horse and stood on the ground, pointing his shotgun at the two men. "Goddam Pinkertons!" John said.

The man in the blue suit smiled at Jim. "Which Younger are you?"

"Question is, who are you?"

"Told ya. Cattle buyers."

"How dumb do you think we are?" John said. "You're Pinkerton men."

"I'm Jim Younger." Jim nodded at his cousin. "That's my cousin John. You ain't lookin' for him. He don't ride with us."

"Is that right?" The man in the white suit suddenly pulled a pistol from beneath his jacket.

"Hey!" John Younger said.

The other man pulled out his pistol and shot John Younger through the neck. As John fell back, his shotgun discharged, and the man in the white suit took the blast in the stomach and was knocked cleanly out of the saddle. Jim shot the other man in the side as he galloped away. The man regained his balance and crashed through the woods.

Jim stared at his cousin for five seconds and knew he was dead. The man in the white suit lay just as still as John. Jim turned his horse and gave chase. He was so stunned that he hardly knew what had happened, but as he rode, the hatred began to mingle with his blood until he was in a blind, unreasoning fury. Even his horse seemed to catch the feeling, and before long they could see John's murderer on his horse. The man was bent over the horse's neck, and just as Jim was about to take a shot, the man pitched from the horse and rolled into the bushes. Jim reined in his mount, stopping just as the man struggled to his feet. He was breathing hard, and a bloody hand covered his side.

"I told you he was my cousin," Jim said. "He never rode with us once. Eighteen years old and I got to take him back to his family dead."

The man just shook his head at Jim. "You broke the law."

Jim Younger shot him through the chest. The man fell backward on the edge of the trail.

"There weren't no need for killin' him," Jim said. Once again he fired into the man's chest. "Weren't no need for it." He holstered his gun and rode away.

At the mortuary door, Jacob Rixley took a deep breath. He was not afraid to face things, but he did not relish doing so.

Leland Giles, mortician, stood up from behind his desk. "Good afternoon, Mr. Rixley."

Rixley nodded. "Let's get to it."

"I understand." Leland Giles led him into the back room.

Rixley winced at the smell of embalming fluid. "It really does smell like death," he said.

Giles nodded. He stood next to a slab on which two bodies lay covered by a white sheet.

"I can't see 'em with the sheet there," Rixley said.

Giles pulled it back.

Jacob Rixley gazed down at his men Lull and Wicher. No doubt about it. He hoped that this might change folks' minds about the James Gang, but he'd been around long enough now to know that it probably wouldn't. "It's them," he said.

Giles covered their faces with the sheet. "I'm sorry. Family men?"

"Not that I know of," Rixley said.

"Everybody's got a mother."

Rixley looked at Giles for a moment. He didn't want everything to be so stupid. "People say they got one of the Youngers."

Giles shook his head. "People say they got the *wrong* Younger."

15

Frank James had it bad for Annie Ralston, and every time he saw her it got worse. He was relieved when the gang went away, and Jesse said he performed like a true soldier when they robbed the Farm Trust Bank in Corydon, Iowa. But once Frank had a pocketful of money, he started talking about getting a little farm. When he told Cole he wanted to settle down, Cole told him he was getting "weak-kneed," and that he'd better do some serious thinking before he made a big mistake. Cole also talked him into doing some serious drinking, and by the time they left Bresnahan's whorehouse in Lamoni, Iowa, they were as broke as when they'd arrived in the state. Frank had it just as bad for Annie. In fact, the pain of his hangover was so severe that he told Cole he thought he was getting too old for all this drinking and carousing. Cole didn't talk to Frank for a whole day. But being broke brings men together, and it was Cole and Frank who finally prevailed on Jesse to get the gang to rob the Mitchell and Company Bank in Lexington, Missouri. His pocket full of money once again, Frank set out to pursue Annie Ralston.

Annie's father ran a haberdashery in Olathe, Kansas, and he considered himself a respectable, forward-looking man. He'd fought for the Stars and Bars during the struggle, but now that it was over he did not look back in anger. He tried not to look back at all. He had his sympathies for the James/Younger Gang (which was why he'd allowed his daughter to attend the wedding of

Zerelda Mimms), but he hated excuses, and he thought the one about the war driving the boys to a life of crime was wearing a little thin. He also liked the orderliness of his store and of the life he led, and the gang with their clattering horses and blazing guns filled him with uncomfortable thoughts of anarchy. If any of this new talk about evolution made any sense, it meant that man was evolving away from savagery.

The first time Frank James had walked into Adam Ralston's haberdashery Annie had luckily seen him first. She ushered him out the door and told him to return after supper when her father would be home in his easy chair. It would not have made him happy to see Frank James paying attention to his daughter. Frank did as he was told, and he continued to visit the store every night for a week. He even went to church on Sunday, sitting behind and to the right of the Ralston pew, missing the sermon as he meditated on Annie's alabaster neck. The next night he walked her to her gate, and he believed she would have let him kiss her, but his courage failed him at the crucial moment.

Frank brought a small bouquet of flowers the following night, and he thought Annie looked especially fine. "Eve-nin', Miss Annie." He handed her the flowers.

"Why, thank you, Mr. James," she said.

Frank looked around the store. "It'd be awfully nice to meet you somewhere else."

"I know," she said. "But this is easier. My father . . ."

Frank raised his hand to silence her. "He's right. I'm an outlaw. I drink too much." Frank lowered his eyes. "And I occasionally drift on to houses of ill repute." He looked up to see her blush.

"Is this a confession?" she asked.

"Actually, I was leadin' up to a proposal." His normally resonant voice cracked on the last word.

"A proposal?" Annie Ralston blushed again. "Business or pleasure?"

"I think you know what I'm talking about."

"Any reason I ought to accept this proposal?"

Frank was glad that Cole Younger wasn't watching him. "Only that I truly love you. And I'll treasure you as best I can."

Annie turned and looked out the window. "We'd have to elope."

"That's fine with me," Frank said. "I'm partial to romantic notions and things that smack of high adventure in noble causes." He put his hand on her shoulder and turned her around. "I'll have a buggy waitin' and a preacher ready in Lawrenceville."

"Ask me proper."

Frank stood at attention. "Annie Ralston, will you accept my hand in marriage?"

She smiled. "Even though you're an outlaw?"

"Even though I'm an outlaw."

She stared at him for a moment, then looked around the store. "God knows where it'll lead me, but it's sure to get me out of selling clothes. I accept, Mr. Frank James."

Frank waited a moment, then said, "May I kiss you, Annie?"

She nodded. "I hoped you'd ask me that as well."

16

It was late when Jesse came out of the Mimms farmhouse, and even though he'd shaved and put on fresh clothes, he still felt heavy, weighed down with sleep. His son, Jesse Junior, lay sleeping in his cradle by Zee's side. She sat on the porch, working on a loom. Jesse smiled at her, then stepped off on the grass and walked over to a little tree. He leaned against it and looked out across a field. "I had a dream last night, Zee."

"Me too. Darnedest thing. I—"

"I dreamed I talked things over with a band of angels." Zee looked up from her work. "What were angels doin' talkin' to you?"

"It was just a dream," Jesse said.

"Seems like it took hold of you pretty well."

"They told me I was never gonna die."

The baby stirred and Zee put a calming hand into the cradle. "You believe that, Jesse?"

He turned around and looked at his little family on the porch. "Just a dream, Zee. Just a dream."

Sheriff P. Rowe of Independence, Missouri, knew that the Pinkerton men assigned to that town, Rasmussen and Timberlake, were fed up with his incompetence and his seeming lack of cooperation where apprehending Jesse James was concerned. So when Reuben Askew, a local farmer, came and told him that he'd heard from someone else who didn't care to be identified that both Frank and Jesse James were visiting their ma, Sheriff P. Rowe headed right over to the hotel to give the news to Rasmussen and Timberlake.

The Pinkerton men had just pulled off their boots preparatory to going to bed, but the thought of catching up at last to the famous outlaws nearly propelled them out the door barefoot. Rixley had gone to Kansas City and wasn't due back until the next day. While Rasmussen and Timberlake put together a crude smoke bomb, Sheriff Rowe went out and rounded up a posse of six, and within half an hour the horsemen were thundering down the road toward the Samuel farm.

A mile from the house they slowed their horses, then walked them in slowly while Timberlake gave everyone his orders. He sent two men around the back of the house and put one on each side. The remaining two stood in the front while he and Rasmussen and Sheriff Rowe got off their horses and approached the dark house. The silence scared Timberlake more than anything, so after a moment he set down his rifle and struck a match. He looked to Rasmussen and then to Sheriff Rowe as the two men jacked rounds into the chambers of their Winchesters, then he touched the match to the bomb's fuse. He took a few steps toward the brooding, silent house, then hurled the misshapen package through the large window by the front door. The wavering light gave the room an eerie quality.

Timberlake aimed his rifle toward the door, hearing voices but unable to distinguish words. He hid behind his arm when an explosion tore open the front wall. A woman screamed and Timberlake saw her moving the boy away from the fire. In a minute it was obvious that neither Jesse nor Frank James were in the house. Timberlake, Rasmussen, and Sheriff P. Rowe mounted up and fled with the rest of the posse back to Independence.

Sheriff Rowe gently suggested that the Pinkertons might be wise to continue out of town, and Rasmussen and Timberlake did not take the time to question his wisdom. Nor did they take the time to return to their hotel, but drove their horses on to Lexington. The next night Jacob Rixley met them in the back of one of the town's dingier saloons. He didn't even bother to say hello.

"What the hell happened?"

"I don't know," Timberlake pleaded. "We put a smoker in the cabin, and all of a sudden it blew."

"The only thing we meant to do was drive 'em out," Rasmussen said.

Rixley looked at his two men skeptically. "You sure it wasn't a bomb?"

"It wasn't a bomb," Timberlake said.

"It wasn't." Rasmussen spread his hands in disbelief. "The old lady must've throwed the smoker in the fireplace and the kerosene went up. That's the only thing I can figure."

Rixley nodded. He knew the men were telling the truth, and he was infuriated that the truth should always be so stupid. "I'm being called back to Chicago to explain this." Jacob Rixley downed a double shot of whiskey. "One thing's for sure. You men did a real good job of makin' heroes out of that whole gang."

The Pinkerton men were not on hand for the funeral of Archie Samuel, and had they been in the vicinity they would have had the sense not to interfere. The crowd that walked slowly along behind Archie's mule-drawn hearse was larger than that at Jesse and Zee's wedding, and only a few of the men did not carry guns. Behind the hearse, Mrs. Samuel rode between Frank and Annie, weeping with sorrow and grimacing with pain. She had lost most of her right arm. Jesse walked sullenly beside the wagon, Zee a few paces behind him.

Zerelda Samuel stayed in the wagon when the congregation reached a little knoll and circled a newly dug grave. Bob, Jim, Cole, and Clell spaced themselves evenly around the circle and kept a lookout in case any valiant posse member should make his play for glory during the funeral services.

Frank James leaned on his rifle and stared at the hole in the ground, barely hearing the verses of scripture read by the Reverend Townsend Hoopes. He had not been around enough to get to know Archie that well, so his grief was not overwhelming. He felt bad for his mother, both for the loss of her son and for the loss of her arm. But he somehow knew she'd be all right. She had more resilience than the whole gang of outlaws, and was probably just as tough. Frank's rage at the Pinkertons was dulled by his depression over the gang and their robbing and all it had come to. Whatever fun there had been had gone out of it now, and the threat of death had assumed a more palpable reality, especially now that Frank had a young bride. So far nothing had been said about Frank's life between himself and Annie. But his half brother's death and his mother's dismemberment had certainly put out whatever candle of romance had flickered around the daring deeds of Frank James.

The Reverend Mr. Hoopes concluded a verse from Ecclesiastes, then stood in silence as he gazed around the crowd. He looked at the sky for a moment. "Archie Peyton Samuel was an innocent boy," he said. "It's a sad day when murder is committed in the name of justice. This act tries the forbearance of good Christian men and makes them turn to the Jehovah of the Old Testament." He looked solemnly at Archie's coffin. "We commend this child's body to the ground. His soul belongs to the Lord."

Very few people knew that Cole Younger played the banjo. He had learned as a child, and he sometimes played when he was alone and gripped by a stubborn sadness. He moved from his guard position to an open space a few feet from the grave, where Clell Miller joined him with his fiddle. Bob Younger pulled out his Jew's harp, then stopped next to Jesse. "I told you them night-ridin' bomb throwers wouldn't dare show their faces." Jesse nodded once, and Bob went over and joined the other musicians.

After a moment they began to play, and as they did, Archie's coffin was lowered into the ground. As Frank and Jesse began to shovel rich earth into the grave, the congregation sang their mournful song.

> "Time is filled with swift transition.
> Not on earth a move can stand.
> Build your hopes on things eternal.
> Hold to God's unchanging hand.
>
> Hold to God's unchanging hand.
> Hold to God's unchanging hand.
> Build your hopes on things eternal.
> Hold to God's unchanging hand.

Covet not these worldly riches
That so rapidly decay.
Seek to gain the heavenly treasures.
They will never pass away."

The congregation repeated the chorus and began another verse. They sang lower now, and they began circling
the grave in a line, stopping to pay their respects to Zerelda Samuel, who sat weeping in the wagon.

Jim Younger leaned his rifle against his shoulder and
yawned. The sad music made him tired, and he would be
glad when the funeral was over. As he walked over
toward his brothers he couldn't help running into Ed and
Beth Miller. Jim looked Ed up and down. "You didn't
bring no gun, Ed." He said nothing to Beth.

Ed nodded. "That's right."

"Any special reason?"

"I ain't got no quarrel with them Pinkertons." Ed looked
back at the grave. "I'm real sorry about what happened
to Archie, but since you boys kicked me out you can
fight your own fights."

Jim felt a fleeting moment of admiration for Ed Miller.
At least he wasn't sniveling. He looked at Beth. "That the
way you feel, Mrs. Miller?"

Beth looked at Ed, then back at Jim. "No. It ain't."

Ed shook his head and grabbed Beth's arm. "Let's go,
Beth. I had enough of talkin' with this fella." He began
to lead her down the hill, but she pulled her arm free.

"You go your own way," Beth said.

Ed grabbed her arm again. "You got to learn to mind,
woman."

Jim Younger fingered the trigger on his Winchester.
"Ed Miller."

Ed turned and looked at him.

Jim gestured toward the bottom of the hill. "Start
walkin'."

Ed Miller faced his wife. "That what you want, Beth?"

For a moment she didn't move, then she nodded her
head slightly.

Ed let go of her arm as though he were throwing it to
the ground. "Then the hell with you." He took two steps

backward and pointed at Jim and Beth. "The hell with both of you!" He turned and stomped down the hill.

Jim and Beth stood and watched him go. It was almost as if they were afraid to look at one another.

Charlie Ford and his brother Bob had also made it to the funeral, and they leaned on their rifles until Frank and Jesse had filled Archie's grave with earth and tamped it flat on top. The Fords had gradually positioned themselves between the grave and Mrs. Samuel's wagon, and as Frank and Jesse walked by, Charlie Ford said, "Awful sorry about your little brother." The James brothers did not acknowledge them. "Sorry," Charlie Ford said to their backs, then looked sheepishly at his brother and shook his head.

At the wagon, Frank put his arm around his mother. "You rest now, Ma. We'll take you back up to Schofield's house in a minute."

Zerelda Samuel looked down at Jesse, tears in her eyes. "Better to lose both arms than little Archie, Jesse. He never hurt no one." She allowed herself a heavy sob. "Why'd them Pinkertons do it? Why, Jesse?"

" 'Cause they thought I was in there, Ma." Jesse stared into the distance, hatred in his eyes. "They wanted to get me any way they could. Men who'd do that are awful low."

Zee leaned against the edge of the wagon, staring at her husband. "You gonna make 'em pay, Jesse?"

Jesse shook his head. "I ain't gonna make 'em pay. I ain't gonna make 'em sorry neither."

Zee looked confused.

Jesse shook his head and gazed out across the hills. "I'm gonna kill 'em."

Zee nodded her head.

17

Jacob Rixley returned from Chicago with orders to lie low. In reality he had no choice. His network of informants had always been thin and unreliable, but after what had happened to Zerelda Samuel it seemed to vanish altogether. He heard an occasional wild rumor that the James/Younger Gang had gone to California or Texas, that they were traveling the country to recruit enough outlaws so that they could withstand an army. Rixley paid it no mind, agreeing with his bosses that an all-out effort to capture Jesse James at this point would be futile. What little surveillance he did have told him that none of the gang members had been near Schofield's house (where Mrs. Samuel was staying) or the Mimms family's farm.

For all Rixley knew, the gang could have been right under his nose. One of the things that irked him most was that he had no idea what any of the men looked like. They were simply names and legends. Even in his sleep, when the outlaws lumbered toward him with guns blazing, their faces were either smooth, featureless skin, or grotesque distortions of a single orifice: a leering, bloodshot eye, a hairy nostril expanding and contracting, a mouth full of rotten teeth and a yellow tongue, roaring with laughter. Once, sitting in a barber shop and watching a stranger have his shoes shined, Jacob Rixley almost called him Jesse. He held back out of a desire not to appear foolish, and that night he dreamed that the man had indeed been Jesse James.

Rixley met with Rasmussen and Timberlake a couple of times, and he finally decided that the two men must be replaced for their own safety. Everyone around Independence knew them on sight, and it would only take a couple of unfriendly bullets to end their careers. The two detectives were anxious to get out and hunt for Jesse once again, but Rixley kept them confined at the hotel in Lexington, and went off to Kansas City to find out about new men.

Although Rasmussen and Timberlake didn't want to leave a job unfinished, leaving was a better alternative that staying cooped up in the hotel. Neither man was a prodigious reader, and neither played chess. Their checkerboard was scarred from overuse, and the Pinkerton men would not have been sad if they hadn't seen another checker for a year. They played solitaire, read the newspaper, and caught up on their sleep, then, after three weeks, they began taking long walks at night when the streets were deserted and businesses closed. No one spoke to them; no one seemed to know who they were, and in six nights of walking they were hindered once by a drunkard and once by an ornery dog.

On the seventh night they went out a little before ten. They went down the back stairs of the hotel, walked through an alley where an old man was playing "Just a Closer Walk with Thee" on the harmonica, then crossed over to the other side of town. Again they walked through an alley, and when they were satisfied that no danger threatened, they went around the buildings and headed down the main street of town. As they passed the hardware store, Timberlake looked in the window and sighed. "You know, I'd really like to be able to go in there and buy something."

"Like what?" Rasmussen asked.

"I don't know. A scythe, a piece of rope. Hell, anything. I think buyin' something would make me feel human again."

"Visitin' that cathouse'd make me feel real human," Rasmussen said.

"Until you ended up with Cole Younger's cousin." Timberlake pointed to the window of the haberdashery. "Look at that." He stopped and pointed at a black suit with thin gray stripes. "I reckon I'd look pretty good in that," he said.

Rasmussen pointed to a hat. "If I wore that I probably wouldn't have to pay in that cathouse."

"Shit." Timberlake spat. "You'd end up payin' double."

Both men turned at the sound of approaching horses' hooves. They looked at each other, but it was too late to run.

The James/Younger Gang spread out in a line in front of them. Jesse drew his pistol. "You boys throwed any more bombs lately?"

Rasmussen raised his hand. "You got it wrong, mister. We didn't do nothin'."

"Sure you did." Cole Younger broke open his shotgun, dropped in a shell, then closed the gun. "A couple of our friends saw you on the North Road that night."

"You boys got one chance," Frank said. "Tell the truth."

The Pinkerton men looked at each other, then helplessly at the outlaws. "We was just following orders," Timberlake said. "Please. It wasn't really a bomb. It was just supposed to smoke everybody out."

Jim Younger cocked his pistol. "One chance out of a hunnert ain't very good odds."

Clell and Bob pulled out their guns and leveled them at the detectives.

"No," Rasmussen said. "Christ!"

Bob Younger grinned down at them. "Maybe we oughta saw off one of your arms first."

"Yeah," Clell said. "Like they had to do with Mrs. Samuel when you got done with her."

"Please," Timberlake said.

Both Pinkertons backed up against the window of the haberdashery.

Jesse James gave them his coldest look. "My little brother was fifteen years old. You think about that. On your way to hell!" He hit Timberlake with his first bullet, then the other gang members commenced firing. The force of the bullets knocked the detectives back through the windows. Both were dead by the time they came to rest amid the broken glass on the floor.

Jacob Rixley pushed through the mortuary door and just stood there glaring at Leland Giles. The proprietor said nothing as he rose and led Rixley into the embalming room. When Giles pulled back the sheet, Rixley held a handkerchief to his face for fear he was going to vomit. The heads of his two detectives were hideously disfigured —they reminded Rixley of his dreams—and were it not for an odd detail here and there, Rixley would not have been able to identify his men.

After a moment his breath came more easily. "Jesus Christ!" he muttered. "What happened to their heads?"

"You got to understand something, mister." Giles covered the men with the sheet. "The Jameses and Youngers are Missouri boys. After they killed your men, they went out and fed 'em to the hogs. Almost ate their heads clean off."

"I can see." Rixley flashed a disgusted look at Giles. "How much do we owe you?"

"Six dollars."

Jacob Rixley paid the mortician, then shoved his wallet angrily back into his pocket. "The funeral will be in Chicago. The governor will be there."

Leland Giles stared at the bills Rixley had given him, then glanced back at the sheet. "I'm sure it cheers their souls just to hear you say that."

"They'd be cheered if they knew how many men we had out combing the hills."

Giles shrugged. "Those boys got a lot of friends out there."

"We'll see how many after this gets out."

Jacob Rixley walked back to his hotel in such a rage that if a man had as much as brushed against him Rixley would have knocked him unconscious. When he got the message at the hotel desk, he bellowed, "Shit!" so loud that the entire lobby grew momentarily silent. The James/Younger Gang had just robbed the Federal Bank of Savannah, Missouri.

Rixley decided that there was no longer any need to play by the rules. All during an obsessed, sleepless night he argued with himself about the methods a lawman should use, and he finally rose at four a.m., lit the kerosene lantern, went to the writing table, and printed in large capital letters across the top of a piece of paper: "LIES, BRIB-

ERY, INTIMIDATION." The words were to become his creed, and he did not give a damn.

For two weeks the newspapers carried stories about the Pinkertons and their devoured heads, fabrications about penniless widows and fatherless children, and blatant exaggerations of the brutality of the James/Younger Gang. At times, as he sat at the writing desk embellishing the tales, Jacob Rixley thought he might have missed his calling. Perhaps he could have been more successful as a writer of romances or as a spinner of tales about desperate men than as a detective for the Pinkerton Agency. Still, his imaginative flights did not cause him to ignore his work. On the contrary, he attacked it with renewed vigor, sending new men into the hills to spread his stories among those who could not read.

His people told him that some folks were turning against Jesse James and his outlaw band, and one night he decided it was time to rub it in. He rode at the head of thirty men, relishing the thought of what he was about to do. At the Mimms farm he had to hold back a smile of pleasure when Beth Miller and Annie Ralston came out on the porch and stood beside the sullen wife of Jesse James.

"What are these two doin' here?" Rixley sat on his horse, illuminated by the torches of the posse.

"Visitin'." Zee stuck out her chin defiantly.

"You got a law against that?" Beth asked.

Rixley gave her a sharp look. "No, ma'am. But we got a law against murder." He slapped his coat pocket. "And I got a warrant."

The three women stared at him, saying nothing.

Rixley shrugged. "It ain't gonna do me any good to ask politely, is it?"

"Ain't gonna do ya any good to ask at all," Zee said.

Rixley caught Annie Ralston's eye. "You the one from the good family?"

Annie swallowed hard. "Everybody's got a good family till they show different."

"Well," Rixley said. "The one you married into crossed over the line. These men of yours are gonna end up leavin' you all alone to think about it." He turned to his posse and pointed to the fields and woods beyond the house. "Just head on through there and fan out into the trees. Get some more torches if you have to." He turned again, tipped his hat to the women, then rode off across the field.

Annie Ralston held back her tears until Rixley departed, but in the darkness of the porch she hung her head and wept. "He's right, Zee. You know he is. Each one of us is going to end up all alone."

"Here, Annie." Beth dried her own eyes and handed Annie a handkerchief. "It'll be all right."

Zee made no move for either one of them, but continued staring out into the darkness. "He ain't right," she said after a moment. "Jesse James ain't never gonna die."

18

Cyrus McCorkindale, a gray-haired farmer in his early forties, strode out of his house as a rooster crowed in the morning. He stopped at the bottom of his porch and watched the sun dancing between the leaves of a few swaying trees, then headed over to the barn and pigpen at the edge of the woods. He carried a bucket in each hand. He emptied one into the outdoor trough as the hungry pigs grunted around it. The other he carried into the barn.

Bob Younger and Clell Miller lay asleep beneath woolen blankets on the floor. Cole leaned against the wall, cleaning the barrel of his shotgun. At the back of the barn, Jesse James was washing up in a large bowl while Frank stood behind him, and in the other corner Jim Younger was brewing coffee. Cyrus McCorkindale shook his head. "You fellas waste the best part of a day." He walked past Clell and Bob and put the bucket down. "Hard to say you was all farm-bred the way you sleep in."

Cole smiled. "Been a while since any of us turned a furrow."

"I reckon." The gang had showed up at McCorkindale's a week before, looking as if they'd been on the run for a week before that. The hills were crawling with Pinkertons and their posses, and McCorkindale hadn't even told his closest neighbor that he was harboring the famous fugitives. A few of the people he knew had begun to lose their enthusiasm about the James boys and their gang, and McCorkindale himself had had his doubts. There was something about making a career out of being an outlaw that he didn't hold with. He'd cheered the James/Younger Gang when they'd started up, cheered them the same as everyone had. But after a while he'd gotten tired of hearing about the banks and the railroads and just wanted to get on with making a living. The railroads had cheated his brother out of some land too, and the boy had gone so crazy with rage that he'd drunk himself to death. But Cyrus McCorkindale wasn't bent on vengeance. He'd picked land far away from where any railroad would want it, close to a waterfall and dense woods, and he raised his pigs and stayed out of other people's business. He let the James Gang stay because he figured his brother would have wanted it that way.

Bob Younger rolled over, and a half-empty bottle of whiskey tumbled out of his blanket. "What's for breakfast?" Bob rubbed his eyes.

"Grits," McCorkindale said. "Cracklin' grits."

"Had 'em yesterday," Bob said.

McCorkindale nodded. "And I reckon you'll have 'em tomorrow."

Clell Miller sat up and yawned, then straightened his battered hat. "Goddam, a man gets hungry."

"I'm sick of this damn hidin'," Bob said.

Cole pulled a piece of cloth out of the barrel of his shotgun. "Who ain't?"

"Mind your manners, Bob," Jesse said. "Just thank McCorkindale here."

"Don't be pickin' on Bob." Jim Younger stared into a cup of coffee.

"Shut up, Jim," Frank said.

Bob Younger jumped to his feet. "Shut up yourself, Frank! I got nothin' but respect for Mr. McCorkindale, Jesse."

Jesse wiped off his face and smiled. "Glad to hear it, Bob." He walked over to the stove and poured himself a cup of coffee. The looks he and Jim exchanged were not friendly.

"I know what's wrong with you boys," McCorkindale said. "You're gettin' the holed-up fever. You need a little air."

"Amen," Frank said.

McCorkindale pulled another bucket off a peg. "I'll fetch y'all some milk after I feed the chickens."

"Much obliged." Jesse James checked his gun for the hundredth time that week. It was still loaded.

McCorkindale stepped into the barnyard and was about to head for the chicken coop when he noticed the hogs milling nervously about the pen. He heard the gun's roar at the same instant that a sharp pain tore through his chest and he was knocked onto his back. He heard more shots, and he rolled onto his side, clawing the earth. He saw one of his pigs take a bullet in the head, but Cyrus McCorkindale died before the pig hit the ground.

Cole Younger had been wounded so many times that he barely flinched when the bullet tore through the side of his shoulder. All he knew was that it would mend if he could get himself out of the barn in one piece. Wood chips were flying around the barn as the bullets came through the walls. Cole protected his chest with an old saddle hanging against the wall, then he knocked out a window and let go with a shotgun blast. He grabbed his Winchester and levered five rounds at the bushes.

"Shit!" Bob yelled. He touched his fingers to his head, and they came away bloody.

"It's just a crease," Frank said as he passed Bob on the way to Cole's side. "Get your gear together." Frank fired a few shots, then tried to protect himself behind a four-by-four as the posse let go with another volley. "There must be a hundred of 'em out there."

Jesse came up to the window by Frank and emptied his revolver in the posse's direction. He couldn't see a thing. He ducked back down to reload. "Jim and Clell, y'all bust a hole in the back of the barn. Then come up here with Bob. We'll all fire after their next volley. Let 'em know we're here."

"They know we're here, Jesse," Cole said. He let go with another shotgun blast.

Bob Younger came up and peered out the window. "What about McCorkindale?"

"He's dead," Cole said.

Frank shook his head. "You can't be sure."

Cole fired again. "He's dead."

"Piss on ya!" Suddenly Frank opened the door and rushed for McCorkindale's body.

Jesse sprang to his feet and followed Frank out the door. "Cover him, damn it!" He fired the Winchester into the bushes.

The bushes answered back, and one of the bullets caught Frank James in the thigh. He spun around, grabbing at his leg, then steadied himself and squeezed off three rounds. He limped the last few steps to McCorkindale, rolled the man over, and listened to his chest. He fired his last three shells, then legged it back to the barn. Jesse followed him inside.

"Well?" Cole asked.

Frank gasped, "You were right."

"How's your leg?"

"Better than your shoulder, Cole."

Jim, Bob, and Clell fired through the windows while the others reloaded. All six outlaws lay flat on the floor when the posse let go with another fusillade. "Lotta kindling on this floor," Cole said.

Clell Miller clenched his fist. "Goddam Pinkertons."

"How'd they know we was here?" Jim asked.

"Maybe you'd like to go ask them," Cole said.

Jesse held up his hand as the firing from outside ceased. "There's a lotta guns out there. We gotta go. We answer their next volley first, then we go. Wounded first. Frank, Cole, Bob, Jim, Clell, then me." He paused for a moment. "We ain't gonna have time to talk when we get to the horses, so I'll say it now. I think we best split up for a while. And that means as soon as we get out of that crick bed. Got it?"

No one said a thing.

The posse fired once again, and once again the James/Younger Gang hugged the ground until the volley was finished. Then they rose and emptied their rifles through the windows and the holes in the barn wall.

"Go," Jesse said. He fired three shots from his pistol before turning away from the battle, and he shuddered at the thought that his outlaw life might be at an end.

Cyrus McCorkindale had built his barn so that it backed up on a steep, woody embankment that ran down to a waterfall and a fast little creek. Ferns grew along the

The Long Riders, left to right, *(top)* DAVID,
KEITH and ROBERT CARRADINE as the Younger
Brothers; NICHOLAS and CHRISTOPHER GUEST as
Bob and Charlie Ford; *(bottom)* DENNIS and
RANDY QUAID as Ed and Clell Miller and STACY
and JAMES KEACH as Frank and Jesse James.

Above: Zee (SAVANNAH SMITH)
and Jesse (JAMES KEACH) discuss
their future as man and wife.

Opposite top: Passengers are held at gunpoint
as Frank (STACY KEACH), left, and Jesse James
(JAMES KEACH), right, rob a train.

Opposite bottom: Trigger happy Ed Miller
(DENNIS QUAID) needlessly shoots a bank teller
during a robbery, thereby jeopardizing the entire gang.

Above: Zee (SAVANNAH SMITH), center, is flanked by Beth (AMY STRYKER) and Annie (SHELBY LEVERINGTON) as she stands up to the Pinkertons' threats.

Opposite top: Jesse (JAMES KEACH) and Zee (SAVANNAH SMITH) are surrounded by friends and family as they cut their wedding cake.

Opposite bottom: Jim Younger (KEITH CARRADINE), left, talks with Beth (AMY STRYKER) and Ed Miller (DENNIS QUAID) who have recently become engaged.

Above top: Jesse James (JAMES KEACH),
left, and Frank James (STACY KEACH),
right, bear somber expressions when they
learn of the death of their younger brother.

Above bottom: Frank (STACY KEACH), left, and
Jesse James (JAMES KEACH), right, defend themselves
in a grueling shoot-out with the Pinkertons.

Opposite: PAMELA REED is Belle Starr, notorious Texas
belle and lover of Cole Younger (DAVID CARRADINE).

Top: Left to right, Cole Younger (DAVID CARRADINE), Clell Miller (RANDY QUAID), Frank James (STACY KEACH), Jesse James (JAMES KEACH), and Jim Younger (KEITH CARRADINE) pause on horseback before riding into Northfield, Minnesota to rob a bank.

Bottom: The James-Younger Gang shoots up the main street of Northfield as they make their escape.

creek, and lots of small caves dotted the embankment. The whole area had been a sanctuary for McCorkindale when he wanted to be alone. It had provided a perfect place for the James/Younger Gang to tether their horses and stow their gear.

As the fleeing desperadoes ran and slid and stumbled down the darkly shadowed embankment, they heard the blast of rifle fire directed against the empty barn. Then the guns grew silent, and the outlaws were left with the sounds of their own heavy breathing and the soft cascade of the waterfall. Frank James ignored the pain in his leg as he balanced himself on a log to cross the creek. Cole came right behind him, his face set impassively against danger and his wound. He jumped to the ground and followed Frank to the little cave where their saddles were stored. The other gang members were not far behind.

"Pinkerton sons of bitches!" Bob yelled while saddling his horse. The gang was out of danger, but a few members of the posse continued firing down the embankment, their bullets striking futilely along the edge of the creek.

Frank James was the first to mount his horse.

"What's it gonna be, Frank?" Cole asked.

"Whole new life." Frank's face actually seemed to be filled with relief. "About time I got to know my bride, I reckon."

Cole snorted and shook his head as he climbed up on his horse.

"How about you, Cole?"

"Time to do a little travelin'. A long way from Missouri." Cole pointed at his little brother. "You come with me, Bob. We still ain't completed your schoolin'."

Bob looked at Jim, then back at Cole.

"Jim's got some things to attend to on his own," Cole said. "That right, Jim?"

Jim sat on his horse, adjusting his hat. "I'll give it a go."

"Where y'all headed, Cole?" Clell asked.

"South."

"I heard a friend of yours went down there."

Cole smiled at Clell. "Come on along if you want to."

"We shouldn't travel too many together," Jesse said.

"You're still welcome," Cole said to Clell.

Clell looked at the ground for a moment, then shook

his head. "Maybe I'll go up North and take a look around. Where you gonna be, Jesse?"

The outlaw leader stared at the waterfall. "Ain't no tellin'. You need to get word to me, you try Mimms' place or Ma's." Jesse James looked at each member of the gang. "We better ride. Good luck to y'all." He turned his horse and spurred it down the creekbed.

Jacob Rixley stood at the entrance to McCorkindale's barn. A whiskey bottle lay on the floor amid the wood chips and spent cartridges and overturned coffee cups. Otherwise there was nothing but a few drops of blood, drops that seemed to mock Rixley by their insignificance. He turned around to face the ample girth of Sheriff P. Rowe. "That's it," Rixley said.

Rowe nodded at McCorkindale's corpse. "Just one. The others broke out the back and got on down by the falls. Guess their horses must've been there."

"Guess that was one part of the planning you missed out on, wasn't it?" Rixley tapped the dead farmer with his boot. "Which one is this?"

"Don't know," the sheriff said. "Never saw this one."

"Well, don't just stand there. Find out who in the hell he is."

19

Jesse James knew that something had gone wrong, but he couldn't understand it. He felt no remorse for feeding the Pinkertons to the hogs, nor did it occur to him that he should feel any. They had killed his innocent half brother and caused his mother to lose an arm. The detectives' fate was no less than they deserved. But now the whole area that had once revered Jesse James turned against him. People didn't seem to care as much about the banks and the railroads and the lost cause of the Stars and Bars. He didn't know who to trust anymore.

One night, not long after he'd gone to bed, he sat up and decided it was time to go. "I'm packin' up, Zee." He climbed out of the soft feather bed. "I got to get away for a spell."

Zerelda Mimms James said nothing while her husband put a few things in his saddlebags, checked his guns, and got dressed. She put on her robe and slippers and followed him out to the barn. Only as he was cinching up his saddle did she say, "Jesse, how long you gonna be?"

"Don't know," he growled.

"Jesse, you know I never tell you what to do. But I don't like this what you're doin' now."

"It's better for you. That's part of why I'm doin' it. It'll be safer for you and the baby."

"I'd like to be the judge of that," Zee said.

"I'll send you money. I'll make sure you get taken care of."

"That ain't it."

Jesse turned on her suddenly. "I'll tell you what's it. The whole country's lookin' for me, lookin' to shoot me down like a dog in the street. I'm tired of duckin', and I don't like sleeping with one eye open. I'm goin' off where they ain't gonna look."

"Must be appealing to think of fading away. Startin' over somewhere else."

"I don't know, Zee. Might just get on with a whole new life."

"Only part that ain't appealing is not bein' who you are." She looked into his eyes. "You sure you're comin' back?"

"I ain't sure of nothin', Zee." He gave her a short kiss on the lips, then swung up into the saddle. "You take care of little Jesse."

He turned his horse and rode off into the night.

Zee leaned against the door and watched him go, and once he was gone she stood there looking at the night. She felt no desire to move, and it was only the cry of the outlaw's son that sent her back inside the house. She took her child from his crib and carried him to a big chair, where she rocked back and forth and cooed a gentle lullaby. It was strange how she seldom felt lonely when Jesse was away. She loved and admired him so much that her thoughts of the man were larger and more comforting than the man himself could ever be.

Frank James' leg healed up fine, leaving him with a scar but no limp. During the two months it took him to recuperate and make his plan, he reread the entire works of Shakespeare and a novel written by an Eastern man around the middle of the century. The book was called *Moby-Dick; or, The Whale,* and Frank James considered it providential that that was the one book Annie Ralston had managed to keep from her father's library. Frank had felt the death of Cyrus McCorkindale deeply, but the image of Ishmael floating on Queequeg's coffin after the *Pequod* had gone down gave him fresh hope. Out of death springs life, and, if nothing else, McCorkindale's death had inspired Frank James to live a better life.

One morning he informed his wife that their last name had been changed to Woodson and that they would depart the following day to take up farming in Tennessee.

Annie Ralston James Woodson had little desire left to remain in the area of Independence, Missouri, and she felt even less inclined to shame herself or her father by coming back to Olathe, Kansas. Deep down she felt that she had made a grave mistake by marrying Frank James. She did not thrive on excitement and danger and legend like Zee Mimms, and she found it difficult to love a man who might be blown down by gunfire at any time. At least the move to Tennessee would be a change, and getting away would probably put them out of danger. Frank seemed resolved to change his ways, and Annie hoped that as time went by she would grow to love him once again. Her major uncertainty was their manner of making a living.

"I don't know a thing about farming," she told Frank as their buggy bounced down a country road on the way to Tennessee.

Frank tipped his hat back on his head and smiled. He was thrilled to be out on the road and getting away from it all. "We ain't gonna be farming, Annie. I told you. We're going to be raising horses."

Annie looked at a swaybacked plowhorse in a farmer's field. "I don't know anything about horses either."

"You'll learn. You know, it's funny. One of the few things I ever really wanted to do outside of bein' a banker or a poet was to raise horses."

"I reckon you're gettin' your chance." Annie's voice was shrewish.

"Everybody's going their own way, Annie. It ain't just us." Frank gestured toward the countryside. "Hell, Jim and Beth are up in the hills somewhere. God only knows where Jesse is. And Bob and Cole are down in Texas. Lord knows why they'd want to go there."

"The only reason Cole Younger went to Texas is that he heard Belle Shirley got married down there."

Frank shook his head. "That's a long way to go lookin' for trouble."

Annie fished an apple out of the basket between her feet. "I should say so. A lot farther off than Tennessee."

Frank put his arm around her. "We'll be all right. You'll see."

"I hope so, Frank." She rested her head on his shoulder.

* * *

Bob Younger had gotten dead drunk in a Dallas saloon during the morning, and had been sleeping with his head on the bar for the better part of two hours when the reporter arrived. Her name was Carrie Simpson, and she was an adventurous young woman on the lookout for colorful stories. She often sought her material in saloons, and she had found many bartenders who were more than willing to give her information.

"I can't tell you a whole lot," Smoky Cullinane told her. He pointed to the comatose Bob Younger. "But this boy's seen his share." Smoky began shaking Bob. "Come on, Henry. Wake up."

"Huh?" Bob sat up and shook his head.

Smoky poured him another drink. "Someone here to see you, Henry."

Bob drank, then stared at Smoky Cullinane. "Henry?"

The bartender gestured toward Carrie. "This here's Miss Simpson, a reporter from St. Louis. I told her you was witness to the James Gang robbery of the Danville train. You remember that, don't you, Henry?" Smoky gave Bob Younger a wink.

Bob thought for a moment, then nodded. "Oh, yeah. The Danville train. Sure. Give me another drink there, Smoky."

Carrie Simpson pulled out her notepad. "Could I ask you a few questions?"

Bob turned on his stool and smiled at her. "Sure."

"Was Jesse—"

"You a reporter?" Bob suddenly asked.

"Yes," Carrie replied. "I'd like to know—"

"That's too bad."

"What makes you think so?"

"It's always sad when a woman has to work."

"I don't—"

"What's the matter with your pa? Not enough money?" Bob Younger took a sip of whiskey and wiped his mouth.

"He's got—"

"Woman pretty as you ought to have a husband." Bob moved forward until his knee bumped hers.

She backed away. "Could we just talk about the robbery?"

"Sure," Bob said. "I'm just sorry to see a woman with a job."

Carrie Simpson let it go. "Did you really see the famous outlaw Jesse James?"

Bob shrugged. "Saw him holdin' the horses."

"What?"

"He wasn't so much." Bob downed another shot. "Frank James neither. I think them Younger brothers really did most of the work."

"Cole Younger?" Carrie wrote the name on her pad.

"Well, yeah. Cole's a pretty tough fella. But the younger Younger brothers seemed like they was in control." Bob Younger leaned back and smiled. "They're a handsome group, that's for sure. All over six foot tall. Much better-lookin' than the James boys."

"Really?" Carrie continued scribbling.

"I wouldn't lie to ya, little lady. That Clell Miller didn't show me a whole lot either. I think Bob Younger was about the toughest, the way I remember. Best-lookin' anyway."

Smoky Cullinane turned away and hid his laughter in a towel.

"I seen that Bob Younger do some fancy ridin', too. Yes sir. Really somethin' the way he boarded that speeding train."

"Sounds like quite a man," Carrie said.

"I hear tell he can drink his share too, and they say he's second to none when it comes to romance." He watched Carrie's pencil move across the white page. "You gettin' all that down the way I tell ya?"

She nodded her head and continued to write. "Certainly," she said. "My paper loves this kind of thing."

Bob Younger continued to drink Smoky Cullinane's whiskey and tell elaborate lies for another hour. It was the whiskey that stopped him, and the next time he woke up his face was once again on the bar. The saloon was crowded and noisy, and when Bob looked to the doorway he saw that it was dark outside.

" 'Bout time you slept it off." Cole Younger looked down at his little brother, then swallowed a glass of whiskey. Cole pointed to a table over in the corner. "Now I just ordered you a nice big Texas steak with some potatoes and succotash. I want you to go over and eat it, and then I want you to go somewhere else and have a big glass of milk. You're gonna hurt yourself you don't get somethin' decent in your stomach."

"Aw, shit," Bob said.

Cole grabbed his arm. "Get goin'."

Bob jerked away. "Don't call fuck with me, Cole Younger! You the one got us down to this place."

Cole nodded. "I know it."

"I'll go eat your goddam dinner and drink your goddam milk, but I'll tell you what, too. Either we do somethin' down here besides wait for your darlin' Belle, or I'm goin' off on my own."

"You wouldn't know what to do."

"I'll figure out somethin' better than this."

Cole slapped him on the back. "Tell you the truth, I've been thinkin' the same thing myself. Somethin' about this situation ain't quite right."

"You said it." Bob stood up and groaned. "I'm gonna start callin' that stool home."

"Go eat your dinner," Cole said.

Cole leaned his belly against the bar and drank two more whiskeys as the saloon filled up and the din of yelling and laughter grew gradually louder. He had been there for an hour when Belle finally slid in beside him. She turned and looked out at the crowd.

"You're late," Cole said.

Belle shrugged. "Never was much for bein' on time." She waved to a man across the room. "You don't look real happy, Cole."

Cole turned and studied the crowd for a moment. "I'll tell you one thing about this Texas. It sure is noisy."

"My, my," she said. "I never figured you for the homesick type."

"I *ain't* the homesick type. I ain't the waitin'-around type either."

"You oughta try gettin' married," Belle said. "Might improve your character some."

"And I ain't the reliable type." Cole looked at the floor

and shook his head. "Where's this husband of yours, Belle? Or did you leave him tied to the bed?"

Belle finished Cole's shot of whiskey. "Don't make no fun of him."

Cole ran his finger over the smooth bar. "Way I figure it is that you probably wear that Indian down, especially with that side swoop and double thump of yours."

Belle glared at Cole. "I do what I want with who I want, and don't make no mistake about it."

"Yeah," Cole said. "That's what people say about you. Always have." He gave her a smile, and she slapped him across the face.

"Now you want to see somethin', just watch." She grabbed the Mexican on the other side of Cole and kissed him so quickly and passionately that the man spilled the drink he had not been able to put down. He did not seem to mind.

Belle gave Cole a defiant look, then kissed the man again.

Cole turned away. "You done yet?"

Belle pushed the baffled Mexican away. "Not by a damn sight." She walked around Cole, put her right foot up on the bar and pulled a small pistol from a band right below her knee. She pointed the gun at the impassive Cole, then she brought it down and shot a glass off the bar. Once again she thrust the stubby barrel in Cole's face, but he never even flinched or blinked. She took careful aim at the cord holding the chandelier and fired. The four-lamped fixture fell to the floor and shattered, and the crowd groaned in awe of the tough little lady.

"Now you done?" Cole asked.

Three bullets ripped through the wooden floor, two on either side of Cole's feet and one right between them. The crowd was suddenly quiet.

"I don't know if she is," a voice boomed from the entry, "but you are."

Cole saw Bob stand up at his table in the back, and he motioned him to sit down.

"Sam!" Belle said.

Sam advanced a few steps, brandishing his revolver. He

wore his brown hair Indian-style, with a band around it. Well-muscled arms hung out of the vest he wore.

Belle ran to him, but he pushed her away and glared at Cole. "You Cole Younger?"

Cole turned himself enough so that he could reach freely for his pistol. "Who's askin'?"

"Sam Starr," the man said. He gestured toward Belle. "I'm married to that lady."

Cole touched the brim of his hat. "Pleased to meet ya."

"No you ain't!" Sam yelled. "I heard a lot about you Missouri boys. Well, I'm from Texas. Father was Irish, ma was a Cheyenne, so I'm born to fight."

Cole nodded approval of Sam's fighting credentials.

"You got a big reputation," Sam sneered, "but you ain't nothin' to me." He looked around the crowd of Texans and grinned. "Matter of fact, the whole state of Missouri ain't nothin' to me." As the denizens of Smoky Cullinane's saloon guffawed, Sam Starr nodded at Cole's gun, daring the Missouri man to draw.

Belle regained her composure and walked between them, a smile of pleasure on her face. "Now, boys," she said. "There's no need to fight over little ol' me. But if you've got to, no guns." She turned to Sam. "Make it man to man." She walked over to the bar and stared at Cole. "Hand to hand."

After a moment Sam Starr shrugged and holstered his gun. "Why not?" He grinned at Cole and pulled out a ten-inch bowie knife. Cole made no move. "I feel sorry for you, Mr. Big Reputation. 'Cause I'm gonna have to carve my initials in your belly." Sam spat on the floor.

Cole sighed. "Glad I caught you in a good mood." He reached behind his coat and pulled out a knife as big as Sam's.

Once again Belle put her foot on the bar and reached under her dress. This time she pulled off one of her long black stockings. She walked between the men as they advanced on one another. "Here you go." She handed an end to each man. "Both of you have a chew."

Sam immediately put one end in his mouth.

"What's the winner get?" Cole asked.

Belle smiled at him. "Nothin' you both ain't already had." She turned and walked to the bar.

"Don't figure, does it?" Cole put the other end of the stocking in his mouth.

"Nope." Belle gulped down a shot of whiskey. "You guys are crazy. But you keep me occupied." She studied the expectant faces of the men in the saloon. "I am having a real good time."

Smoky Cullinane knew that Belle would pay for her damages, so he poured her another shot of whiskey. He had seen five men die in his saloon over the past few years, and each time it seemed to get a little more exciting. It sure broke up a working man's day.

Bob Younger had been about to go get his milk when Sam Starr entered the saloon. As the fight began, Bob had a moment's worry that the muscular young Indian would be too much for Cole, but the first time Sam lunged, Cole dodged with the cat-quick reflexes he had never lost, and Bob Younger put his worries away. He rose from the table as a man in front of him said to another, "Ten bucks on the half-breed."

"I'll take that bet," Bob said. By the time Sam and Cole had thrust and parried four more times, Bob Younger had bet his last hundred dollars on his older brother. He watched the fight for a few minutes to study Cole's technique. Cole didn't miss a thing, but he didn't take any foolish chances. He let Sam Starr be the aggressor; soon enough he'd make a mistake.

Bob Younger studied the face of Belle Starr, and it seemed to grow more sad-looking with every grunt from the two men on the floor. Bob still couldn't figure out what Cole saw in this woman. She was smart and spunky and knew how to show a man a good time, but that didn't mean you rode five hundred miles to see her. Most women Cole wouldn't ride across the street to see. Well, it wasn't anything for Bob to worry about. Frank James had often said that life was a mystery, and Bob believed he'd heard Clell Miller echo Frank's wisdom. He just hoped that when the fight was over they could go back to Missouri.

Sam feinted at Cole, then tried to lunge before he'd completely recovered his balance. Cole was able to knock both Sam's arms out of the way, and suddenly the half-breed spat out Belle's stocking as his face contorted in a grimace of pain. Before he fell, Cole took the bowie knife from his hand. His own was three inches deep in Sam Starr's thigh. Cole sheathed Sam's knife behind his back, then looked over at Belle. The color had drained from her face, and Cole thought that he actually saw tears coming to her eyes. He opened his mouth, and the stocking fluttered to the floor. "What's the matter?" he said to Belle. "You got what you wanted." He eyed her for a moment, then turned and walked out of Smoky Cullinane's saloon. Sam Starr held his leg and watched Cole Younger go.

Outside, Cole stepped into the street and breathed deeply three or four times. He whirled at the sound of boots on the sidewalk, but it was only his brother Bob. "Forgot you was in there," Cole said.

"I never got around to that milk, but the dinner was pretty good." Bob slapped Cole on the back. "Fight was pretty good too."

"I expect it was." Cole had not been so confident about the outcome as Bob.

"Well," Bob said. "What's next?"

"Don't know."

"Want to head back to Missouri? Maybe Jesse and the boys are ready to start ridin' again."

"We'll go back to Missouri. But by way of New Mexico. Still a few places I want to see. We're gonna need some money too."

"Money?"

"Cash money," Cole said.

"I thought you had a bunch of money put aside."

"I spent it."

"On what?" Bob asked.

Cole nodded at Smoky Cullinane's. "What do you think?"

Bob Younger shook his head in disbelief. "You mean you were payin' her?"

"Shee-it!" Cole said. "You don't know nothin', do ya? That woman ain't never given anything away. That's why I liked her. That's also why I'm broke."

Bob reached into his pocket, fished out fifty dollars, and

gave it to Cole. "That's half of what I won on your fight back there. Reckon you're entitled to it."

"I reckon so." Cole pocketed the cash. "Let's ride, little brother."

"I'm right behind you," Bob said.

"You ride beside me, hear?"

20

The death of Cyrus McCorkindale was another onerous
burden that Jacob Rixley had to bear, but when the
James/Younger Gang disappeared without a trace he felt
like a lover who had been suddenly abandoned. For weeks
he moped around Independence, drinking too much, spending countless hours staring at walls and tabletops, wondering what had become of his outlaws. Yes, he thought of
them as his. And sometimes he thought of himself as
theirs.

He could get no information. For two weeks his men
maintained round-the-clock surveillance of the Schofield
place and the Mimms farm, but both Mimms girls had
disappeared, and no one had visited Zerelda Samuel except for a few neighbors. Jacob Rixley finally called off
his men, and he went to Kansas City.

He tried administrative work, but was too restless to
sit for prolonged periods of time. He pleaded with his
bosses until they let him take work beneath his rank in the
Pinkerton Detective Agency. Sitting sullenly beside the
baggage-car stove, he rode trains into the Dakota Territory
and Nebraska, refusing the tedious games of rummy and
checkers offered by his partners so that he could gaze
out upon the endless prairie and not miss a glimpse of
Jesse James. Neither the famous outlaw nor any anony-
mous or would-be brigand attempted to waylay any train
upon which Jacob Rixley rode, and finally he went back
to Kansas City, where at least the chair he sat upon was
cushioned.

His only trip to Independence brought him some hearsay that Jim Younger had moved into the hills—exact location unknown—with Beth Mimms Miller. Two weeks later, as Rixley sifted through the insignificant and repetitive papers that came across his desk, one item stirred his brain and got his imagination working again: Ed Miller had run amok while drunk in Sedalia, and was presently confined to the county jail. Jacob Rixley spent a sleepless night and was on the road to Sedalia before sunup.

As he rode, Rixley tried to stifle his feelings of compassion for Ed Miller. The man had certainly been plagued by bad luck and trouble. It was enough to be thrown out of the James Gang and disowned by your own brother. But then having your wife taken away by another member of the gang was a little too much to swallow. It was no wonder that Ed had become a drunken lout, first drinking and gambling away his mediocre farm, then drifting from odd job to odd job, always quarreling and being fired or stomping off in rage at some imagined slight. Ed Miller's life had not been easy, but that wasn't Jacob Rixley's lookout. He needed what information he could get, however he could get it.

He arrived at the Sedalia jail a little after lunch. A sleepy turnkey led him down a long dark hallway, and the two men peered through a barred window before the door was opened. Beyond, Ed Miller paced in one of the three cells, the jail's only resident. The turnkey did the job for which he was named, then elbowed Rixley as the Pinkerton detective was about to walk through the door. "If you ask me, someone ought to cut that boy's head off. I think he'd hurt a whole lot less."

"Much obliged," Rixley said.

"It's nothin'. Just holler if you need me."

Rixley nodded and walked through the door.

Ed Miller glanced at him for a moment, then hung his head and returned to stalking the perimeter of his cage.

"Ed Miller?"

"You know damn well it is," Ed said.

"My name's Jacob Rixley. I work—"

"I know what your job is," Ed snapped.

Rixley smiled. "What are you in for, Ed?"

Ed stopped his pacing and stared at Rixley. "Bustin' up more than I could pay for. I reckon you know that too. Now what do you want with me, mister?"

"I'm lookin' for Jesse James."

"You and three hundred others."

"You know where he is?"

Ed Miller smirked and shook his head. "And how would I know that?"

"You used to ride with 'em."

"Years ago. I don't know nothin' about them boys."

Rixley gripped his own lapels. "You know Jim Younger ran off with your wife."

"So?"

"Bet you'd like to see him run in."

"It's over, man. Shit! That heifer ain't nothin' to me. Jim Younger neither."

"Is that right?"

"You bet." Ed hung his head and gently kicked the unyielding bars of his cell.

"Ed, if you identify the James boys or the Youngers it would mean a reward for you."

"How much?" Ed asked, not looking up.

"Couple of thousand."

Ed Miller laughed in Jacob Rixley's face. "I got a question for ya. How do I identify what you can't catch?"

"They'll get caught," Rixley said. "Sure as hell. They're done with you, Ed. Even your brother is. You don't owe them boys nothin'."

"And I'll tell you somethin', sure as hell. If I turn 'em in, I'll get killed by some relative of theirs." Ed gestured around his cell. "I got six months left to go in this place, and I'm gonna stay here and then take my chances." He drew his face up close to the bars and scowled at Jacob Rixley. " 'Sides, Jesse might change his mind, an' he pays better wages than you do. Pinkerton man!" Ed Miller lay down on his cot, folded his hands behind his head, and stared up at the jail's ceiling.

Jacob Rixley returned to Independence that night, and he headed straight to the saloon to slake his thirst and ease his troubled mind. He was out of leads once again, and if someone as low-lifed as Ed Miller refused to turn informant, Rixley wasn't apt to find someone who would. As the first swallow of whiskey burned down his gullet, Jacob Rixley nodded his head and decided that he was going to put in for a transfer back to Chicago. He wanted to get on a case that he could solve, pursue men that he could bring to justice. He wanted to do something neat and clean that didn't take forever. Christ, I'm sick of Missouri, he thought.

"Mr. Rixley?"

The Pinkerton man looked up suddenly, then exhaled in relief. It was only the smiling reporter from the New York *Herald*.

"We met a few months back," Carl Reddick said.

"I remember."

"Mind if I sit down?"

"Long as you don't get too comfortable."

Reddick seated himself and pulled out a pad and pencil. "Like to ask you a few things for my newspaper."

Rixley nodded.

"Mainly I'm wondering why you're having so much trouble bringing in the James/Younger long riders."

"Real easy question."

Reddick shrugged. "The people want to know."

"Ah, the people." Jacob Rixley smiled. "Of course. Well, there's lots of reasons." He drew himself up seriously. "I started out with four men who didn't know the territory. You probably know that they got murdered." He let it sink in for a moment. "And down here a lot of people are related to each other. They don't cotton to Yankees from Chicago."

"New York either," Reddick said. "But what about the local police?"

"They get tired and quit after a few miles of the chase." Rixley sighed. "And then there's always the newspapers. Printing lies about the gang, saying that they're Robin Hoods and all. That doesn't help a whole lot."

"Do you know where the gang is now?"

Rixley eyed Reddick for a moment, then looked down

at the table. "We got a pretty good idea. We'll bring 'em in before long." Rixley finished his glass of whiskey.

"The next question I'd like to ask you is about the bomb you Pinkerton men tried to use on Jesse and Frank."

Jacob Rixley stood up and put on his hat. "Goodnight, Mr. Reddick." He strode out of the saloon.

21

After Zee moved away from the farm to St. Joseph, Missouri, she spent a lot of time sitting on the porch. It was a nice place for little Jesse to play, and as the house was only half a block from the main street of town, the porch provided Zee with a spot for daydreaming while she observed the bustle of city life. She went by the name of Mrs. Howard, and she kept pretty much to herself, finding, as she got older, that she needed less and less in the way of human contact. Her boy was a handful, and once she had finished tending to her household chores, she felt no desire to talk to anyone. She couldn't tell the truth anyway. To those who inquired, she simply replied that her husband was away on business. If she was pressed as to what business, she would say, "Farming and cattle. To tell you the truth, I don't know what it is most men do," and leave it at that.

More than anything, she relished rocking back and forth, watching the street and daydreaming about her Jesse. Often men turned their horses from the main street and drove past the "Howard" house, and Zee would study them and wonder when the famous outlaw Jesse James would ride up.

When he did come she barely recognized him. He was riding a big horse as always, and he still wore a black hat with a high peak, but the man had a beard, and she'd never pictured Jesse that way. She went in the house to make herself some tea, and when she came back out her

115

husband was standing on the porch, wearing the smile she
would never forget.

"Hello, Zee," he said.

She looked at him apprehensively for a moment, then
broke into a smile herself. "I kinda like the beard."

"That all ya got to say?"

"You been far, ain't you, Jesse?"

"New Mexico Territory, California. All over, Zee."

"My, my." She envisioned him on his horse, plodding
over immense landscapes.

"Ain't no place better'n Missouri, Zee."

"Are ya back?" she asked.

"Don't it look it?"

She smiled again. "I know you're here, Jesse. I just
don't know if you're stayin'."

"I'm here, Zee. And I'll be stayin' most of the time."

She nodded. "Your son's sleepin' in his crib. He's a lot
bigger than when you left. I expect you'd like to see him."

"I expect I would." He kissed her before they entered
the house, then held her in his arms for a moment. "It's
good to be home, Zee."

When Jesse James saw his son, he got in a real playful
mood, a mood that extended through dinner and beyond,
until he and Zee were at last in bed together. Later, as
they lay side by side, Zee squeezed his arm. "Everyone'll
think of you as Mr. Howard, and if you go out of town
we'll say you're on business or visitin' kin."

"Speakin' of that, did you have any visitors while I was
gone?" He pinched her behind under the blankets.

She smiled. "You mean did anybody come pokin' around
wantin' to fluff up your pillow and straighten the sheets?"

"Just askin'," Jesse said.

"You mind your manners, hear? Just 'cause you fight the
railroads and banks don't mean you get a free tongue
around here."

Jesse stared silently at the ceiling for a moment. "I'll
be startin' that again, Zee."

"Never thought you wouldn't."

"Probably be goin' on a mission pretty soon. Soon as I
can round up some boys."

"Cole and Bob still gone away. Least that's what Beth told me. Jim might go."

"I think I'll try some other folks this time. Just till the old gang gets back. I want to try to build up a little army, a real fightin' unit."

"You must've dreamed some big dreams out on that desert, Mr. Jesse James."

Jesse nodded solemnly. "I did, Zee. I truly did. But it's what I was meant to do. I met this Indian woman, and—"

"Indian woman?" Zee propped herself up on her elbow. "What were you doin' with some Indian woman?"

"It weren't like that, Zee. She was tall as Clell Miller and weighed half a ton."

"Then what was you doin' with her?"

"Listenin'."

"Listenin'?"

"She told fortunes from lookin' at your hand."

"Oh, Jesse." Zee turned away.

He grabbed her and turned her back, his face deadly serious. "Now you listen to me, Zee. This woman had wisdom, and I know it. She had no idea who I was, and she told me things about myself she had no way of knowin'."

"Like what?"

"Like I couldn't change what I was, even though I might've wanted to."

"I—"

"Just listen. I was thinkin' real hard about becoming somebody else. A farmer or a cattleman or an owner of a store. I even thought about becoming a preacher."

Zee gave him a look.

"I did a lot of thinkin', Zee, and I believe at times I was inspired. Now I ran onto this woman somewhere in the New Mexico Territory, way up in the mountains it was. She told me about all that I was thinkin', and then she told me I was wrong for thinkin' it. She didn't know what I was, but she said that I knew, and that that's what I had to be. She said something else that I'm not sure I understand, but I think I do. She said that some men are bigger than themselves, and that for men like that there's

no escapin' what they are. It's almost like they're pre-
ordained."

Zee was serious now. "What did you tell this lady,
Jesse?"

"I thanked her for helpin' me to make up my mind."

"You made it up?"

"It came clear to me right then and there. She said it
would've happened sooner or later without her, that that's
the kind of man I am."

Zee said nothing.

"You're not scared, are you, Zee?"

"No, Jesse. I ain't scared."

"Good."

"You want to know somethin'?"

"Sure do."

"I could've told you everything that woman did. I've
knowed that all along. I never had any doubts about you.
But I knew you had to find it for yourself."

"You!" Jesse covered his face with his hands. "You're
always surprisin' me, Zee."

She snuggled up against him. "They say that's what
keeps a marriage alive."

"I reckon so," he said. "I reckon so."

22

Annie Ralston James was sitting on her rickety porch darning one of her husband's socks when she noticed the buggy coming up their road. She could not distinguish the faces of the four passengers, but as the buggy drew closer she recognized the men, and her heart sank a little further. It didn't have far to go to reach rock bottom. She and Frank James had been in Tennessee for two years, and Frank's dreams of raising horses had long ago been dashed. He hadn't reckoned on the expense, nor had he calculated the disadvantage at which his lack of knowledge put him. He had tried to hide from the reality of failure in drink, and only Annie's strength had brought him around. He still took an occasional glass, but for the most part he worked hard at what he had become: a subsistence farmer with no great expectations.

There were times when Annie thought so seriously about leaving that she actually rose and went into the rudely furnished house to begin packing her things. But she took seriously the words "for better or for worse," and by now she was resigned to stand by Frank James no matter what. She knew that she'd probably always regard herself as cheap and shabby, but she also knew that that sentiment was a result of her upbringing. She took some comfort from the fact that Frank had managed to remain on the right side of the law, but as his brother stepped out of the buggy into their front yard, she trembled with fear that the outlaw call had come again at last.

"Afternoon, Annie." Jesse tipped his hat.

She nodded at him slowly, then turned to the screen door beside her. "Frank, Jesse's here. Him and some friends of yours."

The other men mumbled greetings as they climbed out of the buggy.

Frank burst onto the porch, a big smile spread across his face. The smile faded when he looked down and saw his brother standing with Ed Miller and Bob and Charlie Ford.

"Mr. Woodson of Tennessee," Jesse said. "Gentleman and horse breeder."

"It's been a while," Frank said.

"Brought along the Ford boys," Jesse said.

Frank nodded at the brothers.

"Hello, Frank," Charlie Ford said.

"Good to see ya again, uh, Mr. James."

Frank couldn't tell if Bob Ford was making fun of him or not.

"You remember old Ed, here." Jesse slapped Ed Miller on the back.

"Used to be your brother-in-law, didn't he?"

"Frank."

"I remember Ed, Jesse. They pulled up Missouri and he was under it."

"You be friendly now, Frank," Jesse said. "Ed's company. We took a train to Knoxville and then rode all the way out here 'cause I got something I want to talk over."

Frank looked down at the men his brother had brought with him, then glanced at Annie. Her look was as cold and remote as a mountain peak in the middle of the night. She turned and went into the house.

"We need you back with us, Frank," Jesse said. "We got plans. Ain't that right, Ed?"

"Sure is." Ed Miller reached into his pocket. "We got somethin' to show you." He pulled out a wad of money and waved it at Frank.

"Jesse'n us did the Otterville stage," Charlie Ford said.

Jesse nodded. "Two thousand. Didn't take more'n a couple of minutes."

"We're gonna take the Glendale train," Ed said. "And that's only a start. You with us, Frank?"

"I gotta do some chores." Frank grabbed a bucket by

the door and stomped down the steps. He put his face right next to Ed Miller's. "Ed, you touch any of my liquor and I'll cut your hands off." He strode past him.

"You best mind what he says, Ed." Jesse James followed his brother across the yard.

Frank pushed through the gate to one of his pens and began hurling handfuls of grain onto the dirt to feed the chickens, turkeys, ducks, and geese.

Jesse followed him in and stood behind him. "Place is lookin' good."

"Place looks like shit, and you know it," Frank said. "I gotta leave anyway."

"That right?"

"I reckon. I don't know. Pinkertons been around, askin' questions."

Jesse shrugged. "Least your leavin' fits in with our plans."

"I don't know." Frank would not look at his brother.

"You ain't got no money and you gotta run," Jesse said. "Might as well come with us."

Frank suddenly slammed the bucket down in the middle of the pen, scattering his meager brood of fowl. He turned and gave Jesse a baleful stare. "What the hell you doin' with the Fords and Ed Miller? You've worked with the best, Jesse, and now you're ridin' with the worst."

Jesse gave him a patient smile. "Aw, Frank, they're all right. I made soldiers out of 'em. Discipline. A soldier bivouacs when he's told, marches when he's told, and fights when he's told."

"They're scum, Jesse. They ain't soldiers. Don't you see it? All this outlaw stuff, it's like smoke up a chimney. In a little while it ain't there at all. That's the way we are, Jesse. It's all over. Finished. It got finished at McCorkindale's."

"You know that ain't true, Frank. We did the Otterville stage. Two thousand. We need you on this next one, and I know you're gonna come." Jesse turned and walked back toward the house.

That night after dinner Frank James told his wife that he'd be riding off with his brother at sunup. Annie didn't bother to protest. She told Frank that she'd clean up the business with the farm, then go back to her father's. She said that if Frank wanted to be with her again they'd have to do some talking about the rules. Frank understood. She did the dishes while Frank packed his things, then they crawled into the lumpy bed that had been theirs for two years.

"How many men courted you?" Frank asked.

Annie was surprised at the question. "I don't know. A few."

"Lots of them?"

"Maybe. What's it matter, Frank?"

He shrugged. "I don't know. Just wondered, is all. A man usually asks that of his wife, and I realized I never had."

Annie smiled. "Only one was special, besides you. A cavalry officer with Shelby. Jonathan Catlow. He swore he loved me and said if I ever married anyone else he'd ride off the highest cliff he could find. Well, he ended up riding into the Yankee guns at Chickamauga. Silly, sweet Jonathan Catlow. He was sentimental, like you." Something occurred to her suddenly, and she looked at her husband. "Why didn't you keep your sword, Frank? It's not like you not to have kept it. You must have looked very dashing."

"Didn't have one to keep," Frank said. "When you rode with Quantrill there weren't any uniforms. Just a bunch of old gray dusters. Wore farm clothes under 'em. We were real rag-tag."

"Funny," Annie said. "So hard to picture it that way."

"You're the one that's sentimental," Frank said.

"Was sentimental."

Frank nodded. "Why'd you marry me?"

Annie twisted a lock of hair around her finger. "I don't want to talk about it."

"We're goin' in different directions, Annie. You want the storybook and I just want to be left alone."

"You're right, I guess. Can't help what we want, can we?"

"I don't want no dreams," Frank said. "I had the taste of them and I can't chew 'em anymore."

Annie looked at him with surprise. "Then why are you riding with Jesse again?"

"He asked. And he's family." Frank rolled on his side and faced away from Annie. "It's got nothin' to do with dreaming big dreams."

Annie looked at her lock of hair and smiled. "Can't help wantin' what we want, can we?"

Frank grunted his assent, then reached up and snuffed out the bedside candle.

23

Frank James was not dreaming big dreams as he sat in the passenger car of the Glendale train. But even though his stomach felt hollow and his hands had begun their nervous, pre-robbery sweat, he was happier to be sitting where he was than inhaling the stench of his sorry farm. He was also relieved to be beyond the accusing eyes of his wife. He did not try to fool himself with the notion that he was robbing the train for her; he was doing it for himself, pure and simple, to give himself the necessary capital to get out of his rut and make a fresh start. If Annie wanted to join him again when he was ready, that would be fine. He thought he still loved her, or he thought it was at least possible to love her once again. In truth he had been too poor and worried for the past year to think about love. Had he remained a hardscrabble farmer, he was certain that love would have become as remote to him as the most distant star out in the heavens.

The train began to slow, and Frank James looked up from his paper. Jesse nodded at him from the other end of the car, and both men stood up. An old conductor with a big gray mustache approached Frank, and the elder James brother tipped his hat and smiled before pulling out his pistol. "You just sit down and stay nice and quiet." Frank offered the man his seat.

"What the hell you talkin' about?"

"You heard me," Frank said.

"Well, I'll be!" The conductor shook his head and looked at a couple across the aisle as if to beg corroboration of Frank's lunacy. The couple were terrified. The conductor looked at Frank as though he were an errant schoolboy. "Now you put that gun away and let me collect my fares."

Frank had had no notion that he would meet up with anyone like this, and for a moment he didn't know what to do. As other passengers began to stand up, Jesse James stormed down the aisle, brandishing both pistols.

"Everyone quiet down, damm it!" He held his gun to a man's face, and the man sat down, shaking.

"Just sit down and shut up," Frank said to the conductor.

The old man turned away. "I don't take orders from no bandits."

He began to push past Frank, but Jesse raised his pistol and shot the conductor in the back. Two women screamed, but otherwise the car was silent save for the rhythmic click of the wheels on the track. Frank stared at his brother in disbelief.

"Now come on!" Jesse yelled at him. "Let's get these people's money." He pushed Frank ahead of him, then fired another bullet through the roof of the car. "I want everybody's money in that grain sack, and I mean everybody. Anyone holds back and they'll get the same thing as the conductor." Frank held the sack as Jesse nearly shoved him down the aisle.

As they neared the end of the car, a porter came through the vestibule. When he saw the James brothers he tried to back up, but Jesse reached around Frank and knocked the man out with a pistol butt to the head.

"That's enough, Jesse!" Frank said. "Jesus! That's enough."

"You're talkin' soft, Frank."

They stepped into the vestibule, and for a moment Frank looked at his younger brother. "Why'd you have to kill the conductor?"

"What's it matter?" Jesse said. "He works for the railroad, don't he? Come on."

Jesse stepped to the express-car door and looked through the thick glass beyond which two guards sat playing cards. Suddenly he smashed the glass with one of his pistols and pointed it menacingly at the guards. "Any of you think it's worth dyin' for the Rock Island and Pacific?"

The cards flew out of the men's hands, but in a moment one guard said, "No," and the other shook his head.

Jesse flung open the door, and he and Frank entered the car. Jesse held one gun on the guards, and with the other he blasted the lock off the strongbox on the floor. "Get it, Frank."

Frank dropped to his knees and scooped the money into the grain sack. By the time he had finished, the train had nearly stopped. "Let's go, Jesse." He opened the side door and jumped onto the track.

Jesse backed to the edge of the car, his pistols still pointed at the guards. "You boys sit tight, and you'll have a nice, long life. And you can tell your children that you saw Jesse James in the flesh." He gave a little laugh and jumped out of the car.

Bob and Charlie Ford held the horses, and as the train halted Charlie smiled at his younger brother. "Right on the dot. These James boys is somethin', ain't they, Bob?"

"I reckon," Bob said. "But I can't say as holdin' these horses is so much fun."

"Fun'll come later, Bob. Right now we're earnin' a livin'. That's what's important."

Ed Miller ran up from the direction of the engine and mounted his horse.

"How's that engineer?" Bob Ford said.

"Lookin' for some toilet paper, I reckon," Ed Miller said. "That or a corn cob."

They all burst out laughing as Frank and Jesse approached.

"How much y'all get?" Bob Ford asked.

Jesse swung up on his horse. "We got enough."

"We got it all," Frank said, and climbed wearily into the saddle.

Bob Ford drew his pistol and fired into the air. "Well, let's ride, then. I wanna see my share."

All but Frank fired their pistols into the air and let go with rebel yells as they turned and rode off into the night. Frank knew the good old days were over, and he told himself that this was just a job and that he couldn't think about it any other way.

Rain began to fall as the gang made their getaway, and in an hour, when they reached their hide-out deep in the woods, they were all drenched, tired, and foul-tempered. They stood in the darkness inside the cabin while Jesse fiddled with the lamp, listening to the rain pelt the roof and leak onto the floor.

"That was a hard ride," Charlie Ford said.

The wick caught, throwing a pale light through the greasy chimney of the lantern.

"Well, Charlie," Frank said, "you know how it is bein' out on the trail and all. You probably ain't rode this hard since you robbed that church in Joplin."

"Hey, Frank." Jesse sat down at the makeshift table and began to divide the money. "No need to pick on Charlie."

Frank walked to the door and looked out on the rainy night. After a few minutes he said, "Who the hell built this cabin?"

"Don't know," Ed Miller said. "What's the take, Jesse?"

" 'Bout five grand."

"Maybe it was kin to the Youngers," Bob Ford said. "They all over, ain't they?"

"You ain't got to be talkin' about them," Ed Miller said.

Jesse James stood up and pocketed a wad of money. He walked around the room and gave each man a pile of bills. By the time he sat back down at the table, the others were all staring at him.

"This here's only five hundred dollars." Ed Miller fanned the air with his money.

"Me too," Charlie Ford said. "What is this?"

"The way it is, is what." Jesse shook his head at Charlie Ford.

"What about the five thousand?" Bob Ford said.

"You held the horses. Five hundred's plenty."

"I didn't hold no horses," Ed Miller said. "I got on that train and took the engineer."

Jesse shrugged as though Ed's deeds were nothing. "I planned the holdup. I keep half."

Again Frank went to the doorway and looked out at the rain.

"When did you change the way we split?" Ed Miller asked.

"When I reorganized things." Jesse looked down at the table. "Things are different now."

Ed nodded. "Real different."

Bob Ford took a step forward. "I don't like it."

Jesse James sprang to his feet, grabbed Bob Ford by the collar, and slapped him twice across the face. "You'll like what I tell you to like." For a moment he stared at Bob defiantly, then he let him go. "Maybe next time you can get on the train and earn some more. Now get out of here." Jesse turned his back on the Ford brothers. "I'll let you know when I need you for another job."

Ed Miller stuffed his money in his pocket. "Don't bother callin' on me, Jesse. I'm done ridin' with you." He started for the door, but stopped in front of Frank. "You can keep your whiskey too, Frank."

Unable to look Ed Miller in the eye, Frank watched the drops of water falling into a small puddle on the floor.

Outside, Ed mounted up, then sat in the saddle while the Fords shuffled out of the cabin and climbed on their horses. "You boys gonna ride with him again?" Ed asked.

"Don't know yet," Charlie Ford said. "Only if we get an even split."

"Shit." Ed spat on the muddy ground. "Good luck on that. Somehow I don't think ridin' with Jesse James is such a good idea anymore."

"At least it's a living," Charlie said.

"I used to think so too." Ed began to turn his horse.

"Where you headin', Ed?" Charlie asked.

Ed shook his head in the rainy darkness. "Don't know. But I'm gettin' out of here. Maybe go on to California. This Missouri ain't never been nothin' but grief for me. I'll see you boys around." Ed Miller crashed into the woods and disappeared.

Bob and Charlie Ford headed in the opposite direction, plodding slowly along the slippery trail. They rode in silence for half an hour, and finally Bob Ford said, "You got any thoughts, Charlie?"

"Nothin' good, Bob. Sorry to have to say it."

"Hm," Bob Ford muttered.

"Why?" Charlie asked. "What're you thinkin'?"

"I'm thinkin' that I don't like bein' humiliated. Even by Jesse James."

"Don't worry it too much, Bob. Feelin'll pass."

Inside the cabin, Jesse James lay his head on the table and seemed to fall asleep instantly. Frank watched him for a few minutes, but his own fatigue was so great that he finally found a dry spot on the floor, put down his bedroll, and fell asleep himself. He dreamed of hearing the string band in Olivia Twiss' whorehouse. When he awoke it was light outside, and Jesse was staring at him from the table.

Without a word Frank got up and put his gear together. He went outside and took a good strong piss, then stopped to study the water trapped in a spiderweb on a bush. When he walked back in the cabin he scowled at his brother. "Come to a pretty pass, ain't it, Jesse?"

"I don't want to hear it, Frank."

"Well, you're gonna hear it! It looks like you took a bad turn and never found the way back to the road."

"Why's that?" Jesse stood up. " 'Cause I chiseled them bastards out of a little cash?"

Frank shook his head.

"Or is it 'cause you didn't get what you wanted?"

"You don't see it, do you?"

"What?" Jesse snarled.

Frank threw up his hands in despair. "Sure I'm mad about not gettin' a fair cut. And I think you coulda done better by them boys too. At least told 'em the truth straight off. But that ain't what really gets me, Jesse. It's the whole way you are lately. Like you're an animal that don't know no boundaries. It ain't the way we started, Jesse. It ain't the way we planned to be."

"Aw, shit." Jesse walked past Frank, out of the cabin.

Frank followed him. "Sometimes what people think you are is bigger than who you are."

Jesse turned and faced him. "Folks put a handle on you and it makes you special. Interesting part is finding out how special you are. Or if you are."

Frank shook his head and looked down at the ground.

Jesse took the money out of his pocket. "Go ahead, Frank. Take what you want."

"That ain't the point," Frank said.

Jesse counted off some bills. "At least take what's yours."

Frank shrugged and took the money.

"I ain't crazy, Frank." Jesse came over and put his arm around his brother. "Things is just messed up. Maybe it was ridin' with them scum. Wasn't like the old days."

"You got a wife and son, Jesse."

Jesse nodded. "I reckon I better get back to St. Jo and take care of 'em for a spell. I'll get somethin' else cookin' real soon. You wait."

"I'll be waitin'," Frank said.

The James brothers mounted up. "Frank?" Jesse said.

"Yeah?"

Jesse smiled. "You're a good brother to me, Frank."

Frank shook his head as they rode off down the muddy trail.

24

For a while Jesse James did not know what to do. He went back to St. Joseph to Zee and little Jesse and took up the life of the responsible patriarch. He and Zee bought some new furniture, and Jesse spent two entire weeks putting a fresh coat of white paint on their house. He was not secretive with the few townsmen who occasionally stopped to chat with him, but neither was he gregarious, and his remote manner discouraged people from prying into his affairs. To those who asked, he said he was involved with some Texas cattlemen. Why didn't he live in Texas? What man in his right mind would leave the sovereign state of Missouri?

Painting gave Jesse time to think, and virtually all he could think about was another mission. He needed one badly, for the Glendale train robbery had left him feeling incomplete and dirty. He had lost his head, something a leader could not afford to do, and he had even tried to shortchange his own brother. He had no regrets that Ed Miller was probably gone forever, but he wished he hadn't been so hard on the Fords. Maybe they weren't the most high-class boys around, but they'd shown signs of becoming good soldiers. No matter. Jesse knew he could use them again when the time was right, but what he wanted now was a group of seasoned professionals who could skillfully pull off a job. He wanted the old gang back together.

Clell Miller proved to be the angel of mercy. He rode down the street one day while Jesse was sitting on the

131

porch dreaming of old robberies. Jesse saddled his horse
and followed Clell out of town. The two outlaws sat
beneath the branches of a weeping willow at the edge of
a small stream, and after three hours of conversation the
men went their separate ways. Jesse's mind had not been
so active since he had been driven from McCorkindale's
barn.

That night he lay in bed staring at the ceiling. One of
his arms was around Zee, but it was as though she weren't
there.

"Where are ya, Jesse?" she asked after a while. "You
mind lettin' me in?"

He turned and kissed her cheek. "Thinkin' about my
mistakes, Zee. And how I'm gonna change 'em."

"What mistakes?"

"Last time out, I rode with the wrong people and did
some things I shouldn't have done. But that's all changin'
now that Clell's been here. That boy impresses me more
and more. Don't know where his brother went wrong."

"You goin' away again, Jesse?"

He nodded slowly. "The word's goin' out to the rest.
Cole and Bob are on their way back. We'll be meetin' up
real soon and going on a mission. Real military."

"Right away?" Zee asked.

He smiled at her. "I'll be around for a few days." He
kissed her again, then turned away and gazed off into
space. "From now on things is gonna be real military,"
he muttered.

Beth Mimms (she was now officially divorced from Ed
Miller, and had taken back her maiden name) fell asleep
within half an hour after she and Jim had made love.
Her arm lay across his stomach. For a while he tried to
sleep, even though he knew he couldn't. Finally he slid
out from beneath Beth's arm, put on his undershirt and
pants, and walked out on the Mimms farmhouse porch.
He knew he was taking a chance by even being at the
farm, and he wondered if a Pinkerton man lurked behind
a tree, waiting to end his life. Jim picked the tree that he
would have hid behind had he been a midnight assassin,
then walked to the thick oak and urinated against its trunk.
"So far, so good," he muttered on his way back to the

porch. He leaned against the railing and chuckled to himself.

Tomorrow he'd be joining up with the gang again, and thinking about it made him more excited than he'd been in a while. Jim had been at a point where he'd begun to wonder where his life was going. He'd tried farming and hadn't taken to it too much. For a while, when Beth had to go off to tend to one of her sick aunts, he'd actually gone to Kansas City and worked in three different stores, each for over a month. A store wasn't such a bad thing, he thought, if you owned it. Working in one was like being stuck in the mud. If he made enough from this bank that Clell was talking about, maybe he'd open his own store. Some kind of hardware, probably. Maybe he'd look up Vernon from the Little Rock stage, and they could outfit miners together. Jim would not have minded seeing Vernon's wife again.

Truth was, he was plain restless. He liked Beth well enough, but he didn't know if he was cut out for full-time domestic life. Part of him was always itching to be somewhere else. But he knew he was getting old, and he knew that a man couldn't spend his whole life gallivanting around the countryside robbing trains and banks and stagecoaches. Cole had done a pretty good job of it, but his body carried the scars of about fifteen bullet wounds. Jim didn't think he'd be lucky enough to live through that many.

He jerked upright when he heard a squeak, then turned to see Beth walk onto the porch. "You scared me," he said.

"I woulda knocked, but I was comin' out." She slid her arm through his and leaned against him. "You countin' them stars?"

"Ain't likely," he said. He pointed up to the heavens. "But there's a ring around the moon. Means rain's comin'."

"Maybe you oughta stay."

He shook his head. "No need you bein' up, Beth. Go back to sleep. I got to ride."

"I'm up now," she said. "Won't sleep when you're gone anyway."

Jim looked at her skimpy nightgown. "Put on some clothes then."

"Who's to see me? Besides, you already seen all I got to hide."

Jim looked back at the moon and shook his head. "Ain't right."

Beth laughed. "My, my. Ain't we got high morals all of a sudden."

Jim said nothing.

After a moment, Beth said, "If you ain't countin' the stars, what are you lookin' at?"

"Just the night and the dark. I'm just wonderin' about things, Beth."

Again there was silence. "Jim Younger," Beth said, "I don't know what it is, but you always make things hard for me. Truth is I always did like you, and I just wanted to tell you that before you go off."

Jim turned to her and smiled. He had always prevented her from talking seriously about the two of them. He didn't want to make commitments he would have to break. "Hey, Beth, I always liked you too. And I think you know it, even though you never heard the words."

She nodded.

"We just had some trouble workin' out the timing and all." For a moment he studied the circle around the moon. "I'm gonna go take this bank with Jesse and the gang, get me a little cash ahead. Then I think I'll start lookin' around the state of Missouri to find me some little gal to marry."

"Any prospects?" Beth asked.

"I'm lookin'." He put his arm around her and held her close to his side.

All during the ride to the waystation near Excelsior Springs where the gang was supposed to gather, Jim Younger worried that Beth was going to think he had proposed to her. He needed a drink more than he needed to talk with Jesse James, so after a few words of greeting, Jim hurried into the saloon and downed several shots of whiskey in quick succession. The spirits helped to take his mind off Beth, and so did the incessant monologue of the only other customer at the bar. The burly man's name was Bumper Lewis, and his subject was horses, a subject as dear to Jim's heart as that of women.

"Three things mark a runner," Bumper proclaimed. "Shoulder, placement of the cannon bone, and hindquarters. No horse ever ran worth manure without straight placement of the cannon bone." He touched Jim's arm. "You ever see Gimcrack run?"

" 'Course I did." Jim swallowed his drink and ordered another. "Won the Fairgrounds three years ago."

"Four years ago," Bumper Lewis corrected. He raised his finger like a preacher at the key point in his sermon. "Now Gimcrack had that blaze, which is always a good sign. But the conformation of the hindquarters was somethin' to behold. His turdworks was packed."

Jim raised his hand to silence Bumper. "Mister, you want to start talkin' about conformation, then we better not forget Riddlesworth. I'd have to say that Riddlesworth, the way he was trained for the '69 State Fair, was the best I ever saw." Jim leaned over and breathed his whiskey breath into Mr. Lewis' red face. "Matter of fact, he could've taken Gimcrack at an even swing of the weights."

Bumper Lewis shook his head. "I seen Riddlesworth too. Have to say I thought Castaway in '73 was better. Point is, neither one could hold a candle to Gimcrack."

"I don't reckon I can buy that." Jim looked over at the door as two of the meanest-looking men he'd ever seen walked into the saloon. He thought he recognized them as old friends of Frank's and Cole's—maybe from the Quantrill days—but he could put no names with the faces. He nodded at them and they nodded back before going to a table in the rear.

Bumper Lewis tapped Jim's shoulder to get his attention. "Mister, I don't give a shit what you're buyin'. I'm tellin' you what I think, and I know horses."

Outside, Frank James and Clell Miller were trying their horses to the hitching post as a stagecoach clattered to a halt beside them. Bob Younger jumped out with a big grin on his face. Clell looked at Frank and said, "Looks like Bob boy's started shavin'."

Frank guffawed and slapped Bob on the back. He nodded at the elder Younger as Cole stepped down from the stage. "So how was Texas?"

"I'll tell you how it was," Bob said. "You know what a midget is, Frank?"

Frank shook his head.

"Nothin' but a Texan with the shit kicked out of him."

The four outlaws began walking toward the saloon. "Glad you been workin' on that sense of humor, Bob," Frank said.

"Where you been, Clell?" Bob asked.

"Up yonder north." Clell's nod took in northern Missouri and Alaska.

"You goin' Yankee?" Cole asked.

"Ain't likely."

"How's them women?" Bob asked.

"Husky and healthy." Clell smiled and put his arms around Cole and Bob. "Corn-fed."

Jesse James nodded his approval as the men reached the porch of the saloon. "Good to see you boys back together again."

"How's the family?" Cole said.

Jesse eyed him for a moment, then smiled. "Little Jesse's fine, Zee too. You still Belle Starr's boy?"

"Think I got her out of my system." Cole Younger wiped his mouth on his sleeve. "Let's have a drink to make sure it sticks."

Inside, Jim Younger had been shaking his head for thirty seconds while Bumper Lewis sang the praises of Gimcrack. Finally Jim said, "The Gimcrack you're talkin' about and the Gimcrack I saw run sound like two different animals."

Bumper spread his hands in dismay. "How many times I got to tell you, plowboy?"

Jim Younger did not like being called a plowboy. "I can't say as I'd believe a man who thinks Castaway was a better horse than Riddlesworth."

"Shit," Bumper said. "Ain't no doubt about it." He sipped from his glass of whiskey and leered at Jim.

"Strange," Jim said. "Strange the way two people don't see a thing the same way. 'Specially horses. Guess that testifies to the wonderment of nature."

"Or some people's stupidity."

Jim pointed at himself. "You wouldn't be talkin' about me, would ya?"

"You don't know nothin'," Bumper said. "You're just a dumb shit Missouri sodbuster with puke for a backbone."

Jim smiled at the rest of the gang as they entered the saloon, then turned back to Bumper. "Mister, I'm afraid you're gonna have to take that back."

"Sure thing," Bumper said. "Right away." He grabbed the whiskey bottle off the bar and smashed it against the side of Jim's head.

Jim stumbled backward, staring at Bumper Lewis. Then he shook off the blow. "You hadn'ta ought to done that." Before Bumper could raise his arms Jim had hit him three times in the face. Jim ducked two punches, yanked the portly Mr. Lewis off his seat, and hit him in the stomach with all his might. Bumper doubled over, then fell to the floor after Jim smashed his fist into his cheek. "My name's Jim Younger, and I know about horses."

The gang gathered around as Jim drew his gun. "Now I want you out of here, and I want you high-steppin' all the way."

Bob Younger pulled out his pistol too. "Aw, shit," Bob said. "Let's kill him."

"Let him walk out." Cole Younger gave both of his brothers a stern look.

"What're you talkin' about?" Bob asked.

Cole eyed Bumper for a moment, and Bumper's face was a mixture of hatred and fear. Then Cole looked at Jim. "You took care of him. Now let him walk out proper."

Jim nodded slowly, then eased down the hammer of his gun. He gestured toward the door. "Go ahead on," he said to Bumper Lewis.

Mr. Lewis wasted no time leaving the waystation saloon.

"What the hell was that all about?" Bob asked.

"You run him out," Cole said, "and he'll come around again and try to back-shoot ya. Give him a little room to breathe and he'll be out braggin' that he took on the Youngers. Won't matter that he lost."

"Amen," Clell said. "Now how about that drink?"

When the long riders were all served, Clell Miller

raised his glass. "Here's to bein' together again. May we always ride proud."

"May we always fart loud," Bob Younger said.

The James/Younger Gang drank and guffawed. When their drinks were finished, Frank James pounded his glass on the bar. "Now, can somebody tell me where in hell we're supposed to be goin'?"

"Minnesota," Clell said. "Yes sir. Them squareheads got a real fat bank up there. I scouted it out myself. Town of Northfield." Clell grinned at the others. "Got a real nice cathouse outside of town about ten miles. Them girls know how to treat a fella."

Cole and Frank exchanged looks. "Plenty of banks, and cathouses, in Missouri we ain't done," Cole said.

"Cole's right," Frank said. "We ain't discussed it over-much, Jesse. Minnesota's a fair piece off our mark."

"Bank's full to the brim and overflowin'," Clell said.

Jesse nodded. "We'll take Bill Chadwell and Charley Pitts. They're good men."

"I know it." Cole eyed the grizzled outlaws at the back of the saloon. "At least they used to be. But do we need 'em?"

"It's a big job, Cole," Jesse said. "Little backup won't hurt none."

"I still don't know what's wrong with Missouri," Frank said. "Ain't nobody done the same bank twice. What about that? At least we know the country. I still need a lot of convincing."

"I'm convinced," Jesse said. "Ain't that enough? Now, let's vote."

"You vote." Cole Younger turned and walked out the waystation door.

For a moment no one said anything, then Jim Younger ran after his older brother.

He caught up with him not far from the saloon. "Hey, Cole," he said. "Where you goin'?"

"Don't know."

"What's the matter?"

Cole stopped and faced his brother. "It don't feel right, is what."

"It's my life too," Jim said, "and I'm willin'."

"How come?"

"According to Clell, there's sixty, seventy grand up there just waitin' for us. That's enough to retire on, Cole."

"There ain't no turnin' back."

"I don't know," Jim said, "but I wouldn't mind livin' another forty years and have 'Went to Sleep' written on my gravestone. I'm gettin' tired of this chasin' around, Cole. I know you don't like the way Jesse always takes things over, but he's a leader and you ain't."

Cole started to walk again, but Jim grabbed him. "I ain't sayin' you ain't just as good at things as him. Maybe you're better. But you ain't no leader. It don't suit you, Cole. Jesse knows how to run a group, and he does it better than anyone I knowed of since Quantrill."

"You're workin' me," Cole said.

Jim nodded. "Sixty grand and make it the last raid, huh? I swear, I'm gonna go down to Virginia or the Carolinas, change my name to something I can remember. Buy a few acres or a little store of some kind."

Cole said nothing.

"Let's go out big, Cole. This'll be the last one for all of us together."

"Maybe," Cole said.

"For me, Cole," Jim said.

"That ain't fair."

"For me, Cole."

"Shit." Cole Younger smiled at his brother. "Let's go vote for Mr. Jesse James."

They walked down the street and into the saloon. Cole strode right up to Jesse and looked him in the eye. "You get any dissentin' votes?"

"Not a one," Jesse said.

Cole glanced at each one of the outlaws, then smiled at Jesse. "Guess it's unanimous then."

Jesse nodded and raised his glass. "We move out Tuesday morning."

25

As the train rolled north, Jim Younger sat by the window, watching the night go by. He wondered if he'd been wise to plead with Cole so strongly, but every time he considered the money, he put away his doubts. He figured that the least he'd walk away with would be seven or eight thousand dollars, and his take could possibly run as high as ten. What a man could do with that! He could pretty much call his life his own. He listened to Bob's energetic twanging of his Jew's harp, then he elbowed his little brother in the side.

"Hey, Jim! I'm playin'."

"Take a break."

"What for?"

"I wanted to talk to you for a minute."

"What about?"

"Wanted to give you some advice, Bob boy."

"Shit," Bob said. "Rich as I'm gonna be, I don't need no advice. I just need me ten pretty women to do with as I please."

"That's what I mean," Jim said. "This may be the last robbery for a while, and I was wonderin' if you'd given any thought to what you were gonna do afterward."

"No, I hadn't."

"Don't you think you ought to?"

"Why?" Bob asked. "I'm young."

"Well, what're you gonna do?"

Bob shrugged. "Hang on with Cole, I reckon."

"What if Cole wants to go off on his own?"

"Then maybe I'll go with you."

"What if I get killed or something?"

"What if I do?" Bob grinned.

"You got to think about the future, Bob. You might get a tidy little bankroll out of this job, and you might think about doin' something serious with it. Set yourself up permanent."

Bob stared at his brother, then shook his head. "What's that Beth done to you, anyway? You're talkin' awful strange, Jim. Why don't we just rob the bank, huh?"

"Give it some thought, Bob. This life ain't gonna last forever."

"Don't none of 'em do, I reckon." Bob raised the harp to his lips, then put it down again. "I'll get the money in my pocket first, then make some plans. That suit ya, Jim?"

"Whatever," Jim said.

"Maybe I'll become a newspaper reporter," Bob said. "I met this little gal down in Dallas. She were—"

"Play the harp, Bob," Jim said. "You're right. We'll talk about it when the money's in your pocket."

Bill Chadwell and Charley Pitts had been with Cole Younger and Frank James the first time they'd robbed a bank, before Jesse had become a part of, and then taken over, the gang. The luck of Chadwell and Pitts had never been so good again. Both men had done time in county jails too numerous to remember, and Chadwell had spent three years in the state penitentiary, years that had drained the color from his face and left him with a ghostly pallor. The men had run into Clell Miller when he'd returned from his sojourn north, and Clell had spoken to Jesse on their behalf. Clell himself thought that Northfield might require more than the gang's usual six men, and Jesse, ever anxious to train new soldiers—or, in the cases of Chadwell and Pitts, retrain them—had decided to take them on.

When the men found out the potential worth of the Northfield Bank, they had nearly fallen to their knees and thanked the Lord. Instead, they kept to themselves, not wanting to do anything that would alienate Frank or Cole. Both men had a penchant for strong drink. Pitts had

grown a beard to cover the scars that remained from the
time he'd tried to eat the chimney from a kerosene lantern,
and Bill Chadwell had once run naked through the streets
of Boonville, Missouri, bellowing that a great purple bird
was about to beat him to death with its wings. As a train-
ing measure (and just so neither would miss the robbery
and subsequent division of the spoils), each man had
vowed not to touch a drop until he had departed Minnesota.

Charley Pitts and Bill Chadwell sat together in a seat
near the front of the Pullman car. As the train made its
first stop in Minnesota at the town of Worthington, Chadwell elbowed Pitts in the side. "You ever been up north
before, Charley?"

"Fetterman's as far north as I been." Charley Pitts
stroked his black beard as he contemplated the memory.
"Went there to shoot buffalo one summer."

"How'd it go?"

"How do you think it went, Bill, knowin' my luck?"

"I suppose the price of hides was pretty low."

"Went all to hell," Charley Pitts said. "But I had the
added pleasure of catchin' the clap off some squaw."

Chadwell shook his head. "Reckon you shoulda stayed
home."

"I did till now," Charley Pitts said. "And I'm hopin' I
won't ever have to leave again."

"You and me both."

The train lurched on toward Mankato.

"Pardon me for sayin' so," Clell Miller said to Jesse
James after explaining the lay of Northfield to him for the
tenth time, "but I don't think you need to worry it so
much, Jesse."

"I'll be the judge of that," Jesse said. "This one's gotta
be right, Clell."

"It will be, brother," Clell said. "Them squareheads
don't know from robbin'."

"It'll be nice to get our hands on some of that Yankee
money again. What you gonna do with yours, Clell?"

"Hadn't given it much thought," Clell said. "I was just
thinkin' how nice it'd be to have it. Figured we'd all
keep on going out for a while."

Jesse nodded. "Don't worry about that. I got lots of missions planned. But there's more to life than that, Clell. You ought to think about settlin' down and havin' a family."

Clell Miller looked out the window, then back at Jesse. "I think I gone past that notion, Jesse. Had some bad luck myself, and after seein' what happened to Ed and all, I don't reckon I'll try again. That's not to say nothin' against your sister-in-law."

"That's okay." Jesse wondered where Ed Miller was, and if Jim Younger would be his next brother-in-law. "Man gets lonely in his old age, Clell. Family can be a big help."

Clell shrugged off his fear of future solitude.

"How long you rode with me, Clell?"

"Must be close on seven years."

Jesse smiled. "Guess we showed you some times."

"You boys treated me like family."

"Well," Jesse said, "after seven years I guess you are."

Clell nodded in appreciation.

"Almost," Jesse said.

"You sure do like that readin'," Cole Younger said as Frank James folded the newspaper and put it on the seat.

"It helps pass the time, Cole. Improves the mind too."

"Lotta money that puts in the bank," Cole said.

"No one can take it from you," Frank said.

Cole Younger shook his head and stared out the window.

Frank tapped him on the knee. "Remember that book I told you about, the one where the guy was saved by the floating coffin?"

"You mean the whaling-story one?"

"Well, it was about whaling, but it really wasn't if you know what I mean."

"I don't."

"It doesn't matter," Frank said. "But I read another book by the same author. It was called *The Confidence Man*."

Cole seemed suddenly interested. "About criminals like us, huh?"

"I don't know," Frank said. "It's about a guy who takes

advantage of other people's trust, but it's not really about that either. Most hopeless book I ever read."

"It's about criminals but it ain't, huh?" Cole asked.

"It's hard to say," Frank said.

Cole shook his head skeptically. "I don't know about this author of yours, Frank. Writes whalin' books that ain't about whales, and criminal books that ain't about crime. Sounds to me like the man don't know what he wants to say."

"Maybe I should read them books again," Frank said.

"You do that." Cole leaned back in his seat and gave Frank a wistful look. "You know, Frank, I been thinkin'. When this is all over I just might write a book of my own that'll make me a little more famous."

Frank eyed him for a moment. "If a pig had wings, it'd fly."

Cole ignored the remark. "A book about my exploits as a gentleman. I think I'll call it *My Life* by Cole Younger."

Frank James smiled at his longtime friend and partner. "I expect a free, autographed copy."

"No, Frank." Cole chuckled. "You gotta pay."

The gang remained in pairs after the train stopped in Mankato, buying their horses and leaving town as quietly as possible. They rendezvoused in the woods about fifteen miles south of Northfield in the late afternoon, and Clell Miller eagerly led them up the road five miles to a place where he knew they could pass a relaxing evening. Jesse didn't object. He was tired from their long journey and felt that a good night's sleep would make him just right for leading the gang the next day. He did not worry about their carnal indulgences; everyone seemed a little edgy, and perhaps women could help put the men in the right frame of mind for the mission.

"There it is!" Clell pointed to a large two-story cabin as the gang came around a bend in the road. "These ladies here know how to treat a man."

Two young blond women came out and stood on the porch as the long riders approached.

"Looks okay to me," Bob Younger said.

The men stopped in front of the house. An older woman came out, followed by four more lovely blondes, and bustled down the front steps. She eyed the gang for a moment, then went straight to Jesse James. "Good afternoon," she said.

Bill Chadwell's jaw dropped at the sight of the Swedish beauties. "Will you look at that," he said.

Charley Pitts nodded in agreement. "This trip's lookin' better all the time."

"Them squareheads ain't so bad," Bob Younger said.

Jim Younger, already smiling at one, nodded in agreement.

"We was thinkin' of stopping here," Jesse said to the madam.

She turned and gestured toward the women on the porch. "I have plenty girls. You would like some comfort?"

"Yes ma'am," Cole Younger said. He grinned at Jesse. "Us boys'd like some lodging for the night." Cole dismounted and walked up on the porch. He put his arm around one of the women and turned to face the gang. "I'll see y'all later." He disappeared into the house.

"Much obliged," Jesse said to the madam. He stayed in the saddle as the other outlaws dismounted. "Okay, men," he said. "All I ask is that you go easy on the liquor. I want you all to have clear heads tomorrow." He looked hard at Chadwell and Pitts, letting them know he expected total abstinence from them.

No one said a thing as they climbed the steps to the waiting women.

Jesse James awoke before dawn, had a large breakfast, then stood by the kitchen window with a cup of coffee and watched the sun gradually brighten the gray morning air. Two roosters crowed from the whorehouse yard, and a dozen chickens pecked at the ground. When he heard his men stirring upstairs, he went outside and took a brisk walk down the road.

He told himself that there was no more thinking about the day's job. He had planned as well as he could, and he knew that too much planning could get you in trouble. Each man would be on his own after the robbery and division of the money, and they would all take different trains back to Missouri or ride by different routes. They would reorganize later, and perhaps they'd go after something better than the Northfield Bank. The cities all seemed to be getting bigger, and the banks in those places would make any they'd robbed before seem like chickenfeed. Maybe he'd even take the gang back East, to one of those big Yankee cities like New York or Boston or Philadelphia, and make off with more money than any of his men had ever dreamed about. You had to stay ahead of things, that was the key. Not thinking right was probably what had caused that Yankee general—a man grudgingly admired by Jesse James—to lose all his men to the Indians earlier that summer. If there was an army he could have joined, Jesse might have been out fighting the savages himself.

A pair of cows looked up from their grazing as the famous outlaw walked by. He tipped his hat to them. "Mornin'," he said.

Jim Younger sat on the edge of the bed, pulling on his boots, a satisfied look on his face. He hadn't done any talking with the Swedish girl, but there was little that needed to be said. Jim Younger rose and thumped his chest a couple of times. "That was one fine evening."

The sleepy girl smiled from the bed.

As Jim buttoned his shirt, he said, "I'll be back to see you next time I get around these parts. Honest." He tucked the shirt into his pants and checked himself in the mirror. "I know all the fellas tell you that, but I really mean it." He put on his hat and started for the door. "Take my word."

"*Ta hand om dig*," the Swedish girl said.

Cole Younger said nothing to the naked woman sitting on the edge of the bed. She watched him as he dressed, and he caught occasional glimpses of her in the mirror above the dresser. Cole's evening with her had been pleasant enough, but the truth was that he couldn't get that excited about her smooth, soft, honey-tanned skin. Maybe he'd just give up women altogether, he thought as he put on his hat. About all they did was make him miss Belle Starr, and she was someone he didn't even want to think about, let alone miss. Cole Younger peeled off five dollars and put them on the dresser. He gave the girl another passing glance in the mirror, strapped on his gun, and left the room.

Frank James finished buckling his gunbelt, then gave his girl an embarrassed look. "I used to do this kind of thing quite a bit, but I got married a few years back and it slowed me down a little." He reached for his hat on the bedpost. "You know what I mean?"

The prostitute gave him a blank stare.

Frank shook his head. "You don't understand a word I'm sayin', do ya?"

The prostitute wet her thumb and pretended to count off some bills from a roll. Then she pointed to the dresser. *"Lägg pengarna på byrán,"* she said.

"Yes ma'am." Frank James, thinking himself on the verge of becoming rich for life, dropped twenty-five dollars on the bed, then walked quietly out of the room.

He met Cole and Jim in the hallway, and the three men exchanged smiles as Bob, Clell, Chadwell, and Pitts emerged from the large room they and their whores had been forced to share the previous night.

"Reckon you boys had a mighty cozy time," Cole said.

Charley Pitts stroked his beard. "Wasn't no one but me and her after the lights went out."

"And me and her," Bob Younger said.

Frank looked at Cole and shook his head. "Sounds downright uncivilized, don't it, Cole?"

"I expect so," Cole said.

"Civilizin's one thing I don't need." Bob Younger rubbed his stomach. "Let's get on downstairs and have some breakfast."

The men stomped down the whorehouse stairs.

Jesse James stood in the stable doorway, watching the hired man as he saddled the gang's horses. Outlaw laughter floated out of the kitchen window, and Jesse hoped he wouldn't hear another laugh until the men divided the spoils of the robbery. He took out each of his two revolvers and made sure they were loaded and ready, then he inspected the horses and nodded his approval to the hired man. They each took four horses and led them around to the front of the whorehouse, where they tied them to the hitching post. There was nothing else to do.

In a moment Jesse heard the men coming toward the front door, and he swung up on his horse and settled himself in the saddle. Cole said something as the gang came out on the porch, causing them all to guffaw heartily.

Jesse gave his men a stern look. "I hope y'all had a good time, 'cause we got a busy day ahead of us."

"I'm ready," Jim Younger said.

Bob nodded in agreement. "I stay ready."

Cole smiled up at Jesse James. "How was yours, Jesse?"

"I got other things to think about."

"Family man," Cole said.

Jesse met his smile with an icy gaze. "My family's somethin' you don't talk about, Cole Younger."

Cole's smile faded, and the two outlaws stared at one another.

After a moment Jim Younger said, "Let's just ride on to Northfield and take a look."

Jesse nodded, not taking his eyes from Cole. "Yeah."

"Yeah." Cole Younger turned away and mounted his horse.

26

The gang rode in silence for ten miles, no one wanting to say the word that would provoke an argument and cause the mission to disintegrate before it had begun. Clell Miller led them off the road into a small oak grove atop a rise from where they could look down on the prosperous little Minnesota town. "There she is," Clell said.

A slight wind rattled the oak leaves, and there was a sudden series of clicks as the outlaws checked their guns. The men pulled out their dusters and put them on. Clell eased over between Jesse and Frank and pointed at the town. "Bank's plumb in the center," he said. "Right between the dry-goods store and the mortuary."

Bob Younger checked his Winchester, then slid the rifle into its scabbard. "We're gonna show them Yankees."

Jesse stared at the town and nodded his head a few times. "Okay," he said. "It's gonna be me, Frank, and Clell inside. Bob, you take the north end of town, Jim the south. Cole, you stay with the horses out front and come in the bank if we get in a jam. You're in charge of Chadwell and Pitts."

No one said anything for a moment, then Jim Younger rode around in front of Jesse. "Don't you reckon we ought to send a couple scouts down, check it all out?"

"We rob banks, Jim," Jesse said. "We don't need no checkin'. I got it all worked out. I'd expect something like that from Frank or Cole."

Cole Younger spat at the hooves of Jesse's horse. "I gave up tryin' to talk sense to you a long time ago."

149

"Is that right?" Jesse said.

"Come on!" Clell said. "Let's go down there and take the damn bank. Ain't no one around but a bunch of squareheads."

"Y'all ready?" Jesse asked. After receiving no negative response, he said, "Let's ride!"

As Frank James rode into Northfield with Bob Younger and Charley Pitts, he tried to concentrate his thoughts on robbing the bank. But he kept thinking about what a nice little town it was. The place had a civilized look to it, and the bustling people seemed hard-working and industrious. Still, he turned his horse in front of the bank as Bob Younger proceeded on through town. Frank dismounted and tied up his horse, then looked back across the street to see Charley Pitts sitting on his horse in front of the barber shop. Frank nodded at Jim Younger as he rode through town in the opposite direction from Bob, then the elder James brother walked into the bank as Jesse and Clell reined in their horses outside.

Cole Younger pulled up a little to the side of the bank and watched Jesse and Clell go in. Bill Chadwell had taken up his position near Charley Pitts, and Cole's younger brothers were properly placed at either end of the street. Cole dismounted and began rummaging in his saddlebag and stealing glances at various angles of the town. He'd be glad when this was over and he was back in Missouri. One thing for sure: this was his last ride with Jesse James. Cole allowed that Jesse had some talent to lead, but that didn't mean he had to act like some Napoleon or goddam Julius Caesar. Cole didn't hold with any grandiose notions about himself or the gang. They were just a scruffy bunch of long riders trying to stay a couple of steps ahead of the law and the poorhouse.

Inside, Frank James backed away from a little table when Jesse and Clell entered the bank. At a signal from Jesse, the three men pulled out their revolvers. Frank stepped to the door and slammed it shut. "Okay, let God see the palms of your hands!" He counted seven customers in the bank.

Jesse shoved the cage door open and pointed his pistol

at the cashier, Joseph Heywood. "You don't give us no trouble."

Heywood raised his hands and shook his head.

"Get the vault, Clell."

Clell grabbed Heywood and shoved him over in front of the large black door. He threatened him with his gun. "Now you open that safe or I'll blow your head right off."

"I can't." Heywood's voice was like a squeak, and he coughed to clear his throat. "It's a time lock. It only works at four-thirty."

Clell pushed him against the door. "What're you talkin' about?"

"Time lock?" Jesse bellowed. "Mister, you better open that safe, hear?"

Heywood's hands shook in the air. "The Pinkertons told us you might be comin'. The lock's set just for you."

"What?" Jesse said.

"Really, mister. The whole town's ready."

Clell Miller looked to his leader. "Shit fire, Jesse! What do we do?"

Frank James looked to his brother and Clell for a moment, and a large man in a blue suit and derby hat took advantage of his lack of vigilance and shuffled a few steps toward the door.

Outside, Cole Younger looked up and down the street, then turned to face a smiling, well-dressed man who was wearing a very large black hat. The man patted Cole's horse on the hindquarters. *"Är den här hasten till salu?"*

Whatever it meant, Cole Younger didn't want to hear it. "I'm busy, mister." He turned away, wondering what the hell was going on inside the bank.

The Swede stroked the horse again, then tapped Cole on the back. *"Hördu, jag vill köpa hästen."* He pointed to himself and smiled.

"The horse ain't for sale," Cole snarled. "Now move on, squarehead."

Cole had been aware of a whistling sound that seemed to be getting steadily louder. He bent down to tighten the girth on his horse as the Swede waved some money in his face. *"Hur mycket ska du ha för den?"*

Cole stood up straight and was about to shove the ardent lover of his horse when something else caught his eye. Turning onto the main street was a slow, lurching metal machine, whistling like crazy and blowing out steam like a locomotive. It had large metal wheels, and for a moment Cole thought he had fallen asleep and been given over to nightmares. The machine looked as if it would take forever to make it down the street, and Cole had to fight himself from running into the bank and telling Jesse that the robbery was over and that the gang should get on their horses and ride home. This Yankee ingenuity was too much! At last Cole calmed himself, thinking that the noise might even make the robbery easier. He smiled at Chadwell and Pitts (who were trying to keep their agitated horses under control), then shrugged his shoulders as the tractor coughed its way down the street.

Inside the bank, Jesse walked over to the quaking Heywood and put the cold metal of his gun against the man's head.

"Please don't shoot, mister." Heywood darted his eyes back and forth at Jesse and Clell. "I have a family."

Suddenly a woman screamed.

"Shut up!" Frank said. He did not notice that the burly customer had moved closer to the door.

Jesse took Heywood's chin in his hand. "Now you got five seconds to open that vault."

"I can't," Heywood croaked.

"Four," Jesse said.

Frank James took two steps forward. "Jesus, Jesse."

The man in the blue suit jumped to the door and opened it.

"Look out!" Clell bellowed. He raised his pistol and fired a bullet into the man's back as he stepped out on the landing.

Cole Younger whirled at the gunshot and beheld the bleeding citizen of Northfield standing above him. The man looked at Cole, his face twisted in pain. "They're robbing the bank!" he bellowed.

"What the hell?" Cole muttered.

The man came down one step and stopped. "They're robbin' the bank!" Then he pitched forward and landed in a motionless heap at Cole's feet.

"Jesus Christ!" Cole pushed the confused Swede away

from his horse and pulled his Winchester from its scabbard. "Bob!" he yelled. "Jim!"

He whirled again as the bell in the church steeple began to clang. "Come on, Bob!" He waved at his little brother, then turned to the other end of town. "Jim, move!" He fired two rounds into the air and watched a few people scrambling for cover.

Inside, Frank James put his hand on Jesse's shoulder. "Come on, Jesse. We gotta move. Fast!"

Jesse nodded, and the brothers headed for the door.

Clell started after them, then turned and faced a relieved Joseph Heywood. "Yankee bastard!" Clell Miller raised his pistol and shot Mr. Heywood through the forehead. He ran out of the bank and found the Swede obstructing the path to his horse. Clell shot him down and mounted up. His head was spinning so fast that he thought he was going crazy. It had all looked so easy, and now everything had gone wrong. He saw three men with rifles bolt from an alleyway and barricade themselves on the other side of the main street, and he experienced a fear for his own life that he had never felt before.

When Jim Younger heard Cole's shout, he pulled out his pistol and fired two bullets into the air, figuring that would be enough to strike terror into the hearts of the Northfield citizens. But it occurred to him that he'd never heard Cole yell quite like that, and as he rode down the street toward the bank, he could see that a well-ordered response to the gang was developing, not the panic he had hoped for. As he rode past a side street, a bullet slammed into his left arm with such force that it knocked him out of the saddle.

Jim Younger howled in pain, taking cover behind his horse and firing at the three riflemen behind the barricade. He dropped one, and the other two ceased firing and quickly dragged their wounded comrade to safety. He reloaded his revolver and was about to climb back on his horse when he was knocked into the dirt once more. He felt as though he'd been smashed in the cheek with the barrel of a Winchester, then he tasted blood, and a hot spike went up the base of his brain, and his teeth were like so many marbles in his mouth. Jim put his hand up to his face and realized that the bullet had made a hole in both his cheeks, and for a moment he forgot his pain as he thought of how hideous he must look.

"Can you get on your horse?" Bill Chadwell was a blur beside him, firing his gun at men Jim could not see.

Jim spat out blood and teeth, and when he tried to talk nothing but a gurgle came out of his throat.

"Jesus Christ!" Chadwell said. He bent to help Jim, but the middle Younger somehow managed to mount up unassisted. "Try to follow me," Chadwell said. "We gotta get out of this place." He looked down the street as Bob Younger galloped toward the bank, firing his pistol through store windows.

Cole Younger watched Jim mount up, then watched three new men replace the others behind the barricade on the side street. Men with rifles seemed to be appearing all over the town. Cole put his foot into the stirrup, then fell to the ground as a bullet pierced his other leg.

"You okay, Cole?" Jesse asked.

Both Frank and Jesse were trying to get on their horses, but the gunshots were causing the animals to panic, and they seemed on the verge of bolting without their riders.

"I'll make it," Cole said. He swung up on his horse and fired at the men behind the barricade.

As Clell Miller reloaded his pistol, Frank and Jesse finally made it onto their horses.

"Shit!" Cole Younger grabbed his left shoulder, and blood came through his fingers.

"Got you covered, Cole." Bob Younger whirled his horse in front of the bank and fired at a rifleman on the hotel roof. The man dropped his rifle and stared at the street for a moment, then pitched forward. He bounced off an awning before landing on the street.

"We gotta move, Jesse!" Frank said.

"Okay, okay." Jesse looked around. "North end. Let's ride! Don't bunch up too close."

No one in the gang was much concerned about bunching up or not as they galloped toward the north end of town, firing at the armed townsmen. Cole's other leg was grazed, and Clell Miller took a bullet through the forearm.

Frank James heard bullets whizzing past his ears like incredibly fast bees. He put his head low over his horse's neck, and just as he thought the gang was going to make it out of town, his heart sank. He saw two large wagons blocking the street by the livery stable. "Jesse!" he screamed. "They got us cut off!"

"We gotta go for the other end!" Jesse bellowed. Jesse James did not see how the gang could ride down the street again, but there was nothing else to do. Every side exit was cut off, and if the men stood still and tried to fight, every one of them would be killed. They wheeled their horses around and galloped for Northfield's south end.

"Mother of God!" Bill Chadwell bellowed. He dropped the pistol from his right hand and clutched his chest. He swayed to the side as though about to fall off his horse, and he looked at Frank James with sorrowful eyes. Then he tilted forward again as his horse veered up on the boardwalk. Another bullet smashed into his side, then his face collided with the low-hanging sign of the haberdashery, and he was suddenly flat on his back outside the entrance to the store. Bullets tore into the wood around him, and as he got to his feet he wondered why he hadn't been hit again. He thought that Providence might look out for him this time. Then a shotgun blast hit him squarely in the chest and knocked him through the storefront window.

The gang did not slow down for Bill Chadwell, but rode like madmen to escape the Minnesota town. Cole Younger took another bullet in his upper arm, and Frank's thigh was creased deeply enough to start a slow oozing of blood. Frank James did not cry out over his wound, but when he saw that the south end of Northfield was securely barricaded too, he bellowed, "Oh, no!" with all his might. It was more than a man's sight should have to bear.

Bob Younger screamed in pain as a bullet shattered his knee, and a round that went through Jim Younger's foot nearly caused him to fall out of the saddle. He spat more blood as he wheeled his horse around, and let out a barely audible moan.

"Where the hell we goin'?" Frank screamed, as Jesse led the gang north again.

"Just follow me," the outlaw leader yelled.

Charley Pitts felt suddenly as if someone had driven an

icepick through his forehead. Then his stomach seemed to explode in fiery pain. He bent forward, but was whipped back as his horse accelerated, and he toppled from his speeding animal. Charley Pitts was dead before he hit the ground. His right foot remained in the stirrup, and by the time Charley's horse stopped at the north-end barricade, the street had shaved the rider's face of both beard and skin.

As Frank turned his horse to follow his brother, he caught sight of a man with a rifle on the side staircase of the hardware store. The man raised his gun, but before he could fire, Frank James put a pistol bullet through his throat. The rifleman toppled down the stairs as, once again, Frank raced toward the north end of town. He had no idea where he was going or what he was doing, and he felt completely ruled by blind, unreasoning panic. He was going to die soon, like a man trapped inside a flaming theater with a hysterical mob.

Halfway up the street, Jesse James slowed his horse and veered a little to the right side. He pointed to a large storefront window across the street, then fired his pistol at a rifleman on the roof. The man fell straight through a wooden awning and landed in the splinters on the porch below. "Through the window!" Jesse bellowed.

Jim Younger's face and neck were covered with blood, and his eyes looked as vacant as a dead man's. Frank wondered how he even managed to stay in the saddle. Jim, Frank, and Jesse charged the window side by side, hunching over and closing their eyes as the shattered glass showered down around them.

They just missed a fusillade of bullets, but Clell Miller was not so lucky. As he made his approach to the gaping window he was hit in the chest, the stomach, and the leg. He howled in agony as his horse jumped into the store, and his mind was suddenly awash with images from all through his life. The memories terrified him more than his blood and pain, for he knew the past was flung on drowning men in the same manner before they died.

Cole took another hit in the forearm as he started into the store, then he turned his head in time to see Bob take a bullet in his chest and fall backward off his horse.

The gang plowed through the dry-goods store, overturning tables and smashing glass cabinets, scattering items all over the floor. Jesse and Frank reached the back window first, and as they smashed through it, Jesse's horse tripped on the lower sill, catapulting the outlaw leader into the alley dirt.

Frank James stopped as Jim, Clell, and Cole rode past him. He grabbed the reins of his brother's horse. "You okay, Jesse?"

Jesse leaped up from the ground. He still had no bullet wounds, and he had not even been cut by the broken glass. "Let's go, Frank. I think we can get out of here." Jesse leaped on his horse and headed out of town.

"I'm goin' back for Bob." Cole made a sharp turn down another alley that led back to the main street.

"Cole," Frank yelled.

"Let him be," Jesse said.

Every breath Bob Younger took felt like a stab wound in his chest. Still, he managed to hold onto the reins of his horse, and with his other hand he squeezed off a couple more rounds. He was alone on the street now, and it never occurred to him that he would do anything else but die there. He at least wanted to take a couple more townsmen with him. He fired again, then another bullet ripped into his chest. He tried to scream, but he couldn't take a deep enough breath.

The men guarding the main street whirled as Cole Younger's horse pounded down the alley at them. Before they could aim their guns, Cole had fired and dropped both of them. He turned onto the street and headed for his little brother. Bob lay writhing in the dirt, still holding the reins in one hand.

Bob Younger's pain was so bad that he wanted death and nothing more. He didn't want to lie suffering and alone on the street of the town that had finally routed Jesse James and his famous outlaw gang. He rolled over and squinted through his tears up the street. For a moment he thought he had died already, and then he actually forced a smile and shook his head as he saw his bloody brother Cole riding toward him. He got to his knees, and another bullet hit him in the shoulder. He let go of the reins to cover his wound, then the pain in his chest caused him to slump to the ground again.

"Come on, Bob boy," Cole hollered.

Once again Bob Younger rose to his knees, raising his hand as Cole stopped beside him.

"Shit!" Cole bellowed as another bullet grazed his side, then he bent down and took his brother's hand. He pulled Bob up behind him, simply putting the pain out of his mind as he was hit twice more. He fired shots in different directions. Bob was hit again and slumped against Cole's back, gasping something unintelligible. "Hold on, Bob," Cole said. "We're headin' on back to Missouri." Cole Younger whirled his horse around and galloped for the alleyway before it could be sealed off once again.

Jesse James led Frank, Clell, and Jim down the alley-way. "That's it!" He pointed to a low brick wall between two buildings, and he knew it was the last barrier keeping him and his men in Northfield. He didn't know how Clell or Jim could withstand the jump, but there was nothing else to do. Jesse cleared the barrier first, then Frank. Clell spat up a giant glob of blood as his horse hit on the other side, but he managed to stay in the saddle. Jim Younger's impassive face grew livid with pain as his horse cleared the wall. He rocked in the saddle and seemed about to lose his grip, but then came upright and hung on. The gang galloped past Northfield's outlying houses and finally got beyond the townsmen's bullets.

Cole Younger got off the main street and into the alley, losing the tip of his little finger to a bullet in the process. As he raced toward the end, a man on a loading dock smashed his rifle butt into an underpinning strut, causing barrels and boxes to spill into Cole Younger's escape route. He then fired his gun three times before Cole shot him down.

Cole veered to the left to avoid a rolling barrel. Three townsmen appeared on a roof in front of him, and with his last two bullets Cole hit one and scattered the others. He dug his heels into his horse's flanks, no longer giving a damn for the debris in the road. He had to clear the wall, and he needed speed for that. Even with Bob aboard, Cole's horse jumped the brickwork with room to spare— Cole thought that the Swede had not been wrong in wanting to buy him—and when he landed Bob clutched Cole so hard that the elder Younger had to hold himself back from screaming in pain. Cole thought he must have been wounded in every part of his body, and he could not tell if the blood running down his back came from one of those wounds or from Bob's gurgling mouth. By now they were out of reach of Northfield's guns, and if they could simply keep from bleeding to death, things would be all right. It was hard to believe that they had left only Bill Chadwell and Charley Pitts behind.

Cole caught up with the others in fifteen minutes, and for another fifteen they plunged and crashed through the woods. "We gotta stop," Cole finally said as they came to a small meadow. "My brothers can't take no more of this." It was as though no one else could take any more of it either, and everyone's horse seemed to stop instantaneously. Behind Cole, Bob moaned softly. Everyone stayed in his saddle for a minute or so, breathing heavily and with immense weariness. Finally Cole climbed down.

He rolled out his blanket by a fallen birch tree and gently laid Bob down on top of it. He tore off his shirt and made some bandages for Bob's wounds, but he didn't think his little brother would make it through another hour. As Cole was helping Bob, Jim slid off his horse, stumbled over to the log, and sat down. "Can I do anything for you, Jim?" Cole asked.

Jim gazed off at nothing and shook his head slowly.

Cole Younger sat down between his brothers, too exhausted to do anything about his own wounds. Most of them had stopped bleeding, and he thought the best thing he could do was just lie still.

Clell Miller staggered a few feet, then dropped to his knees and crawled over past Bob to the end of the tree. Sweat dripped off his face, and he spat up a generous quantity of blood before drinking from his canteen.

Jesse helped Frank down from his horse, and the elder James brother grimaced from the pain in his leg. They hobbled away from the Youngers to another log and sat down. Frank dabbed at his wound with a handkerchief, and Jesse stared straight ahead. It was a full five minutes before he turned to Frank and said, "We got to move. They'll get the rest of them to a doctor."

Frank eyed his brother for a moment. "Who will?"

"The posse that'll probably be here in ten minutes."

"We can't do that, Jesse. We can't run out on them."

"It ain't runnin' out, Frank. It's survival." Jesse James stood up and walked across the clearing to Cole.

He looked at Clell, then at the Youngers. "Let's ride, Cole." He gestured at Jim and Bob. "Make the others up comfy, and then let's get out of here. Posse's comin'."

Cole Younger's lips curled in a sneer. "I won't let you do that." He pulled out his revolver and pointed it at Jesse. Blood dripped off his hand and the butt of his gun.

Jesse made no move for his pistol. "We gotta move, Cole."

"What about the rest?"

"They ain't fit to ride." Jesse shrugged. "There ain't time to argue with you, Cole. If you're fixin' to die, you stay. Me and Frank's goin'." He turned away. "You comin', Clell?"

Clell Miller coughed again. He couldn't have risen had he wanted to. "I got us into this," he muttered. "Least I can do is stay." He looked at Jesse, then doubled over in pain.

"Suit yourself." Jesse turned his back on Cole Younger and walked slowly toward his horse.

Cole cocked his pistol.

"Oh, God!" Bob Younger suddenly hollered. "Kill the pain, please." He grabbed at his chest and writhed from side to side. "Shoot me, Cole. Please! Jesus! Do somethin'!"

Cole put his hand on his brother's shoulder as Bob slipped back into delirium. He kept his gun trained on Jesse as he cut his horse from the bunch. Cole tried to focus all the hatred he felt for Jesse James, but he finally did not have it within himself to kill him. He eased down the hammer and lowered the gun, then looked at Frank James. "Frank?"

Frank rose and walked toward his horse.

"You're stayin', Frank," Cole said. "Ain't you?"

Frank put his hands up on the saddle, then looked back at Cole. "Jesse's my brother, Cole. I got to stick with him." He gave a little shrug before turning away and pulling himself onto the saddle.

Cole holstered his gun. "The Younger brothers don't need you."

Jesse turned around and looked at the wounded men. "Good luck, boys," he said. "God hold ya."

Cole Younger spat. "You know, Jesse, I sort of like it this way. I get to watch you run."

Jesse James turned his horse, and he and Frank rode away.

Jim Younger rose up, a faint sign of recognition on his face, then slumped back against the log and cast a dismal stare at the ground.

"I'm here, Cole," Clell Miller gurgled. "I ain't leavin'." Clell fought the air for breath. "Ain't no pain worse'n what I'm feelin' right now. All my fault," he gasped. "I thought it'd be easy."

"Weren't your fault," Cole said. "No one made us go."

Bob Younger stirred, and Cole patted his hand. "Cole, you there?"

"We're all here, Bob boy. How you feelin'?"

"All sticky." Bob coughed and clutched his chest. "The blood's run down in my pants and everywhere."

Cole poured a little water over Bob's lips.

"Goddam squareheads," Clell said. He looked up at Cole. "Goddam squareheads cleaned us out. Who'd've figured it?" He laughed and coughed up some blood. "Jim said this was gonna be the last one, Cole."

"He was right."

Clell held his hand over his stomach and tensed in a sudden spasm of pain. "Goddam squareheads," he muttered, then fell over dead, his face in the leaves and the canteen dripping water beside it.

There was nothing more for Cole to do, so he leaned against the log and stared out at the horizon. "Where the hell's Missouri?" he asked.

Frank and Jesse rode on and on. Frank did not know where his brother came by all his energy. Frank himself lost track of time, and his spirits sank so low that he could barely look up to ascertain the direction in which they were traveling. Not that he cared. Jesse could have led him right to the door of the Mankato sheriff and

Frank wouldn't have minded as long as he was given a bed to sleep on.

He became aware of the darkening sky and felt a little relieved that soon they could stop for the night. They came over a hill and headed down to a wide river beyond which the succession of hills seemed endless. They stopped at the water's edge, and while the horses drank, Frank shook his head.

"We can make it," Jesse said.

"We can't, Jesse." Frank looked beseechingly at his brother. "I can't."

"What kinda talk is that? We done the impossible lotsa times. It's just a little river."

"I'm tired, Jesse."

"You can't quit on me, Frank."

A desperate quality had crept into Jesse's voice, and Frank James thought that his brother must be unutterably lonely.

"Come on," Jesse said. "We'll get us a new gang together. Yeah. We'll get the Ford boys back. Couple of others I know. We justa gotta get across this river, Frank."

"I can't." Frank felt like a weak boy who could no longer keep up with his sturdier comrades.

"Shit!" Jesse suddenly let go with a rebel yell and swatted Frank's horse across the rump. Then both horses plunged into the river and began struggling across.

Frank fought off his initial panic and let the swift water cool his weary body.

"We'll soon get back to Missouri," Jesse said.

"We never shoulda left."

"Aw, Frank. We'll get going again. I gotta keep goin'. You know what I mean, don't you, Frank?"

Frank nodded his head, knowing all too well what his brother meant. Then he said, "It's over, Jesse."

Jesse gave him a sharp look. "Frank, it ain't never gonna end."

27

When Jacob Rixley received word that the Younger brothers had been captured in Minnesota and were on their way to the Stillwater penitentiary, he walked out of his office without telling either his superiors or his subordinates where he was going. He hurried to the Chicago rooming house where he lived, grabbed the bag that he always kept packed, and caught the next train to Minnesota. He did not congratulate himself until the train was safely out of the station.

What he had done was anticipate the outlaws' moves, and he was amazed at how correct he had been. He had known that he would have to wait until they regrouped and pulled another robbery for practice. But once that was done, Rixley figured that they would move on to a different territory and not try the patience of their fellow Missourians any longer. Jacob Rixley was a reasonable man who did not have much use for intuition or hunches. Still, it had been his hunch that the gang would go for one of the richer banks in the north, and he could not reasonably explain why he felt that way. He had begun to notice that older detectives often went with their feelings, and one of them had told him that after a while a detective begins to think like a criminal. Indeed, Rixley had pursued and thought about the James/Younger Gang for so long that at times he thought he could have led them himself. He remembered being surprised that they had picked a payroll as skimpy as the five thousand dollars on the Glendale train. He had alerted twelve towns in Minnesota, Iowa, Wisconsin, and Illinois that their banks were considered prime targets by the gang. He had advised special security precautions at the banks themselves and a well-planned response by the townsmen should the outlaws come. Northfield had been one of the towns, and the people had acquitted themselves well.

All except for letting Frank and Jesse James get away. Well, Rixley thought, you can't have everything. He had Clell Miller dead, and soon he would actually see Cole, Jim, and Bob Younger in the flesh. They would not be on the outlaw trail in the foreseeable future. As for Frank and Jesse James, Jacob Rixley could wait. He was so determined to get them that he could not imagine the capture never taking place. Jesse James was probably panicked now, what with his gang in disarray and all, and he'd probably lie low for a while until he could organize a new group. On the other hand, that same panic could force him into a premature move. With the Northfield failure nagging his pride, Jesse might attempt a foolish robbery with men insufficiently trained. Rixley chuckled to himself as he thought that his advice might be useful to Jesse James. Then he resolved to go straight from Minnesota to Missouri once he had finished grilling the Youngers.

"They're some awful tough men, I'll say that." The warden led Rixley down a corridor that separated the actual prison from the hospital wing. "I think you and I would be dead if we'd gone through what they did. I actually sort of admire 'em. The toughness, I mean." The warden shook his head. "Never thought I'd hear myself say that."

"I know the feeling," Rixley said.

The warden opened the door into the hospital bay. "There they are. Guard'll bring you back when you're ready."

"Much obliged."

"That's Cole in the fourth bed on the left. Jim and Bob are down at the other end."

"Thanks again." Rixley had hoped he would be able to pick them out by himself. The warden left, and Rixley took a few steps into the room. "Jesus Christ," he muttered as he noticed Carl Reddick down at the far end, joking with Bob Younger. Then the Pinkerton detective took a few steps more and stopped at the foot of Cole Younger's bed.

Cole looked at him, and when Rixley nodded, Cole turned back to the doctor as though Rixley weren't there.

"Startin' to look like I ain't gonna die, huh?"

The doctor nodded. "You might make it."

Cole looked at Rixley again. "I still feel awful poorly, though."

"Ain't exactly a surprise. Eleven bullets might be some kind of record."

Cole forced a smile. "Reckon that gives me twenty-six for my career. Or maybe twenty-seven. I kinda lost track."

"No matter," the doctor said. "I don't suppose you'll be adding any more to your total."

"Unless I try to run," Cole said.

The doctor stood up and laughed. "Not on those legs. At least for a while. See you tomorrow, Mr. Younger."

Cole bowed his head. "Good day, sir."

After a moment he looked up at Rixley, who continued to stare at him. "What you gawkin' at?"

"Cole Younger. Lately of the James/Younger Gang."

Cole snorted. "Who might you be?"

"Jacob Rixley."

"The Pinkerton man."

Rixley nodded and sat down in the doctor's chair. "Been wantin' to meet you for a long time."

Cole gazed at the bandages on his chest. "Hope I live up to your expectations."

"You're one person I'd never be disappointed to see. Especially shackled to a prison bed. What happened to the others, Cole?"

"What others?"

"Frank and Jesse. They were the two that got away, weren't they? There were two of them, I know that."

Cole smiled at Rixley for a moment, then closed his eyes and leaned back on the pillow.

"How do you and your brothers feel about a life sentence?" Rixley asked. "You fellas are lucky that this state don't allow hangin'. Real lucky."

Cole grimaced, then moved his arm down and covered a wound on his side.

"Come on, Cole," Rixley said. "Tell me how you feel about it all."

"Oh, I don't know." Cole opened his eyes and gave Rixley a weary look. "We tried a rough game and lost. What more is there to say? I was four years in the war and eleven years gettin' out."

"What about the James boys?"

"What about 'em?"

"They were with you in Northfield, right?"

"I don't know nothin' about them boys." Cole looked over toward Bob and Jim.

"Sure you do," Rixley said.

Cole turned and stared coldly into the Pinkerton man's eyes. "Far as I'm concerned, they ain't never been in this state."

"But—"

"I'm tired, mister. Wounded and tired. I'd be obliged if you let me get some shut-eye."

"But they were—"

"Much obliged!" Cole closed his eyes and turned his head away from Jacob Rixley.

Carl Reddick had positioned his chair between Bob and Jim Younger so that he wouldn't have to look at Jim. Although the middle Younger's wounds were less serious than those of his little brother, his jaw had been shattered and he was unable to speak. Jim's face was wrapped in bandages, and the black circles beneath his eyes made him look as though he'd never known a happy moment. He sat up in bed as still as a statue, staring dejectedly at the thin prison blanket.

Bob, on the other hand, seemed as happy-go-lucky as a schoolboy caught in a prank. Reddick was amazed that Bob could even breathe, let alone talk, after the many wounds in his chest. The doctor felt he should be dead, and was expecting mortal complications to occur at any time. Still, Bob talked eagerly with Carl Reddick, even asking him questions about the journalism business, although his voice was soft and he was often short of breath. Reddick could not help liking the bucktoothed, guileless

Bob; there was something about him that seemed so innocent, something Reddick couldn't figure out.

"Do you feel bad about any of it?" Reddick asked him. "I mean, about all the robberies and deaths."

"I don't know." Bob shrugged his bullet-riddled shoulders. "Guess it's over, ain't it? Don't know what I feel."

Reddick thought that Bob would fit in just fine with prison life. He seemed like the type that would accept whatever happened to be around.

"Me and my brothers are rough boys," Bob said. "Used to rough ways. I guess we gotta abide by the consequences."

Carl Reddick recorded Bob's words on his pad, then looked up for more.

"I guess you could say we was drove to it."

Reddick nodded. "How's that?"

"Sometimes the events is in the saddle and makes a fella turn out a certain way." Bob coughed up a little blood into a dish beside him. "Hadn't been for the war, we might've ended up doin' something else."

"Come on, Bob."

"What?"

"You were a little young to have fought in the war."

"That's true," Bob said. "But my brothers weren't. And we all go in one direction together. We're family." Bob looked up at Rixley as the detective stopped at the foot of his bed. "You another reporter?"

Rixley and Reddick exchanged smiles.

"My name's Rixley, and I work for the Pinkerton Agency. I've been chasin' you for a long time."

Bob grinned and shook his head. "Yes sir. Guess you have."

"I don't mean to interrupt your interview with Mr. Reddick here."

"Quite all right," Reddick said. "I think we're finished."

"What do you want?" Bob asked.

Rixley leaned on the iron railing of the bed. "I want to talk to you about the James boys, Bob. Want you to tell me if they were with you in Northfield."

Bob stared at him, saying nothing.

"You don't owe them a thing, Bob. If it was them, they wouldn't protect you if it got them one day less. If you help, you and your brothers might get a reduction on your life sentences."

Bob whipped his head around as Jim Younger made a gurgling sound from beneath his bandages. Then he turned back and faced the detective.

"What did he say?" Rixley asked.

Bob looked down at the blanket, then back at Rixley. "He said to tell ya we done it for Dixie and not nothin' else."

They stared at each other for a moment, then Bob said, "That's all, mister. I got nothin' more to say to you."

"Where to now?" Reddick asked Rixley as the two men walked out of the Stillwater penitentiary.

"Where do you think?"

"Wouldn't be Missouri, would it?"

"Just might be."

Reddick laughed. "You really think you're going to arrest the James brothers, don't you?"

"I *know* it, Mr. Reddick."

Reddick shook his head. "If I were you, I'd stay in Chicago and enjoy the good life. Someone'll kill those boys sooner or later. No sense in you running yourself ragged over them. What's in it for you? You don't seem like the type that does things for the glory."

"It's in the blood now," Rixley said. "Don't think there's any way I can shake it. Probably like you'd be with a good story. I guess that's why you're here today."

Reddick curled the end of his mustache. "Always good to see you, Mr. Rixley."

The detective shook his hand. "Somehow I don't think it's the last time."

28

As Bob Ford got older he began to think a little more about life, and he wound up thinking that it was a pretty raw deal all around. He'd been losing his respect for Charlie for quite a while, and after the Glendale train robbery Bob Ford decided that he probably had at least as much sense as his older brother. He was angry with himself for not striking back at Jesse James after the outlaw had slapped his face, and he was even angrier with Charlie for thinking that he should have accepted the slap. Well, Bob Ford was learning about things, and he'd learned that you didn't get to the top by letting people slap you around. It wasn't the way Jesse James got there, and it wasn't the way Bob Ford was going to get there either.

What Bob Ford hated most about his brother was Charlie's pride over having helped Jesse rob the Otterville stage and the Glendale train. Sometimes he thought that Charlie would be content to sit around and boast about his paltry deeds forever. And now that Dick Liddell had told them that Jesse wanted the brothers back in his gang again, Charlie was like a pig in shit, saying that riches were just around the corner. Bob Ford leaned against a telegraph pole outside the livery stable. Charlie was inside, betting on the dog fights, but Bob was getting sick of the kinds of men that hung around such contests. He wanted something better out of life, and he felt it was about time for the breaks to go his way. And he didn't know if riding with Jesse James was the smartest thing he could do. Hadn't done Clell Miller and the Youngers much good at Northfield, that was for sure.

In the back room of the livery stable, Charlie Ford elbowed his way to the front of a pack of shouting, sweating men. In the middle of the circle were two black men, each holding a dog by the collar. The dogs' faces were only a foot apart, and the crazed animals yipped and snarled at each other as the members of the audience put down their bets. Charlie Ford studied his thin stack of bills, then signaled a bet to the man holding the scoreboard. Charlie Ford always liked a winner, so he put his money on Mr. McCoole, a five-to-four favorite over Stonewall. "Go for the throat, McCoole," Charlie yelled as the frenzied dogs attacked each other.

Bob Ford listened to the shouts of men desperate for three or four dollars, then looked once again at the poster tacked to the pole above him. It read: "WANTED, DEAD OR ALIVE, JESSE AND FRANK JAMES—$10,000 REWARD." Bob Ford tore down the poster, rolled it up, and walked into the livery stable.

He made his way to the front and squatted down beside his brother. Charlie's expression grew somber as one of the dogs weakened, and when it finally crumpled in a twitching heap, Charlie shook his head in disgust. "Shit!" he said. "That cleans me out."

"No use us hangin' around then, is there?" Bob asked. He took his brother by the arm and led him out to the street.

"Sometimes I don't know about my luck, Bob," Charlie said. "I'd be tempted to say I was on a losin' streak if we hadn't seen Dick Liddell."

"Goin' out with Jesse James just might keep that streak alive, Charlie."

"Whaddya mean?"

"I mean that maybe there's another way to change your luck. Mine too." He unrolled the poster and showed it to Charlie.

"So what? Nothin' new about that."

"Price has gone up since Northfield," Bob said.

Charlie pointed to Jesse's name. "That man's worth every penny of it, Bob. He's the best."

"That man slapped my face."

"He'll make it up to you on the next job. Reckon we ought to head on up to St. Jo, Bob."

Bob Ford shook his head. "There ain't gonna be no next job."

"I'm broke."

Bob pointed to the poster again. "You wouldn't be broke if you had half of ten thousand dollars."

Charley Ford stared at his brother. "I don't know as I like what you're sayin', Bob."

"Well, you better start likin' it. I'm sick and tired, Charlie, and I think it's time I started makin' some decisions. You ain't exactly had the right stuff lately, you know what I mean?"

"I'll grant you that," Charlie said. "But turnin' in Jesse James? Don't you think that's a little risky?"

Bob Ford grinned. "I didn't say nothin' about turnin' him in."

"You talkin' about killin' him?"

"Finally gettin' through to you, ain't I, Charlie?"

"No sir. No sir! We wouldn't last five minutes."

"We wouldn't be around but four. We take care of Jesse, collect that reward, and then it's goodbye, Missouri. And I mean forever."

"Leave Missouri?"

"Shit, Charlie. Don't be so goddam thick."

"But I ain't never been nowhere but Missouri."

"So what? One place is the same as another. Your feet's on the ground, there's hotels to sleep in and whiskey to drink. Probably some better jobs to be had too."

"I don't know, Bob."

"Well, I do! And I'm goin' after Mr. High-and-Mighty. You can come along with me or stay here. It's up to you."

"I'd like to stick with my brother."

"Then let's go. I got things figured out real well. We just got one stop to make first."

Jacob Rixley had resolved to follow up on all leads concerning Jesse James, no matter how dubious they might be. For two months he had labored in futility, and when the grimy note from the Ford boys reached him at his hotel, he had no reason to suspect that it would yield him any positive dividend. Still, he rode up to Liberty to meet the brothers. He no longer minded a meeting that accomplished nothing; rather, he dreaded passing up the opportunity that would lead him to his prey.

He sat in another back corner of another saloon, drinking bad whiskey and waiting. He wondered what kind of life he would lead if he rounded up Jesse and Frank the next day and put an end to his quest. He thought that he would probably be lonely for a while, then perhaps he'd settle into the normal life that most people led—a wife, a family, the little house that he'd been saving for. Or perhaps he'd put his knowledge to use and become a bank robber.

Two men walked into the saloon, looked around, then headed for Rixley's table. He knew right away that everything he'd heard about the Ford boys was true, and he bowed his head to conceal a derisive smirk.

They sat down at the table and stared at him for a moment.

"Gentlemen," Rixley said.

"We're the Fords. I'm Bob."

"And I'm Charlie. You probably heard of us."

Rixley nodded. "Don't you boys have a little pig farm down by Independence?"

"We're—"

Bob Ford reached out his hand and silenced his brother. "Let's just talk business." He pulled the wanted poster from his pocket and rolled it out on the table. "We're gonna get Jesse James for you."

"Good," Rixley said. "The reward is ten thousand dollars."

"We want fifteen."

Rixley studied Bob Ford for a moment. "That's a lot of money. Even the Pinkerton Agency and the governor of this state can't afford that."

"You know who you're talkin' to?" Charlie Ford suddenly said. "You know what kind of men hail from Missouri? The Jameses and Youngers, the Clantons and Earps, and now Bob and Charlie Ford. People gonna know who we are."

Rixley listened politely. "Word is that you and Jesse ain't even friends no more."

"That so?" Bob Ford smiled. "Well, mister, that very same Mr. Jesse James that you can't find at all just asked us to come and visit him." Bob pushed his chair back from the table. "Let's go, Charlie."

"Wait a minute." Rixley put up his hand. He sensed Bob Ford was telling the truth. "How about twelve thousand?"

Bob slapped his palm on the table even as Charlie gave an affirmative nod. "I didn't come here to bargain, mister. Otherwise I woulda started at twenty. Now I want fifteen, and that's it."

Rixley drained his glass. The whole deal suddenly made him sick, the low-down, sleazy way of it. It was the last kind of bargain he ever wanted to make, and yet he knew there was no way out. "Okay," he said. "Fifteen thousand."

"We want half of it now," Bob said.

"I'll have it for you tomorrow morning."

"We'll pick up the other half in Kansas City." Bob grinned. "On our way out of here."

"It'll be waitin' for you."

Bob and Charlie Ford stood up. "Looks like you got yourself a deal, Mr. Rixley," Bob said.

Rixley stared at the table top. "It looks that way," he said.

29

The next day a pair of wealthy Ford brothers rode into
Plattsburg, Missouri, took a room in Binny's Hotel (the
best in town), and spent the rest of the afternoon pur-
chasing the goods that Bob thought fitting for their new
station in life. They bought new suits and shirts and boots,
went to the barbershop for haircuts and shaves, and, in
exchange for their tired nags and quite a bit of cash,
obtained newly shod horses that were swift and strong.
They picked up the supplies they would need on the road
during their escape, and cleaned and oiled their guns in
preparation for meeting Jesse James. After a sumptuous
meal of the finest cuts of Kansas City beef, Bob dis-
suaded Charlie from spending the remainder of the evening at the bar, and the two men retired to their room.
"Liquor dulls the mind," Bob Ford said. "And we gotta
be thinkin' clear tomorrow."

In the room, Bob sat on his bed spinning the cylinder of
his revolver. He felt content, almost as if his job was already done and he had nothing more to do but ride to
Kansas City and collect another seventy-five hundred dollars. "I don't see how nothin' can go wrong," he said.

"I hope you're right, Bob." Charlie stroked his smoothly
shaven face. "I'm a little scared myself, you want to know
the truth."

"I been over it, Charlie. This is gonna be the easiest
thing we ever done."

"What if Frank's there? Or someone else?"

"Frank won't be there. Dick Liddell said he's off in

174

Kansas with that high-class wife of his. And Jesse don't associate with folks in St. Jo."

"Dick said he was thinkin' of bringin' Ed Ryan in to ride with him."

"Whiskey Head Ryan?"

Charlie nodded.

"Shit," Bob said. "Not yet. He'll start with us. We're the only boys he knows that's reliable."

"Guess he'll be happy to see us."

"I expect he will," Bob Ford said. "I'll tell you this— he'd be damn lucky to have us ridin' with him again."

"I guess." Charlie Ford didn't quite see the logic.

Bob Ford grinned. "Too bad he's gonna be dead."

Charlie Ford looked down at the rug and shook his head.

"What's eatin' you, Charlie?"

"It's a big change, and all of a sudden," Charlie said. "What we gonna do afterward, Bob?"

"Head west. Simple enough."

"West is a big place."

"Big enough for us to find a place to settle, Charlie. I don't know. Heard some good things about Colorado."

"I'll leave it to you, Bob. Guess you're callin' the shots now."

Bob nodded. "You just trust me, Charlie. I been thinkin' real hard about things."

"It's a load off my mind," Charlie said.

"Let's get some shut-eye," Bob said.

In the morning Bob and Charlie Ford shaved for the second day in a row, strapped their gear on their new horses, and headed for St. Joseph.

Since he had received no wound at Northfield, Jesse James returned home to St. Joseph with a deepened sense of invincibility. He also carried a profound hatred of the Pinkerton Detective Agency, and the fact that he had not been wounded made him feel that he was somehow destined to take revenge on those insignificant men who had foiled his boldest attempt at crime. He would need a new gang, but he thought that that would come to him in time. He could wait with his family in the meanwhile. Frank was done with him where outlaw missions were concerned, but Jesse accepted that. Frank had never been a leader, nor would he ever be one. He had served his time like a good soldier, and Jesse reckoned that he had the right to retire. Jesse had decided to recruit the Fords again because they had served him faithfully in the past, and he was genuinely sorry for mistreating them.

Jesse had visited his mother once, and she was much better than he had expected her to be. The old farmhouse had been rebuilt, and she was doing well enough to have a couple of men working her fields. She did a lot of visiting around now, because the railroads had agreed to let her ride free for life. She did not need a pass; she would simply wave the stump of her right arm at the conductor, and he would welcome her aboard. Jesse had asked her to come and live with him in St. Jo, but Zerelda Samuel had declined. "I'm too big to share a house with another woman," she had said. Jesse knew she was right, but he felt it was his obligation to at least offer. He took Beth Mimms back with him instead.

As he and Beth rode north, he explained to her how bravely Jim Younger had fought at Northfield, how he had ridden gallantly despite his many wounds, and what a shame it was that Jim would spend the remainder of his days behind the bars of the Stillwater penitentiary. He knew that it would take time for Beth to get over the loss of her lover. Still, life went on, and he thought a woman as pretty as Beth shouldn't hide her light under a bushel. He advised her to get out and meet other men, but when he suggested that she might take the time to get acquainted with the Ford boys, she gave him a hard look and said, "I already know more about those two than I care to know." Jesse James said no more.

He spent most of his time in the vegetable garden behind the house, first expanding it, than planting and watering and weeding. And thinking. He always found it better to keep his hands occupied while dreaming of his future exploits and ruminating on the past. It was too bad about the Youngers and Clell Miller, but their loss was not something that brought deep grief to Jesse James. He thought of himself as a leader, and he thought of his men as soldiers. Soldiers were replaceable parts of a machine, and when they were gone, you found new ones. Besides, he was glad he wouldn't have to deal with Coleman Younger anymore. Cole had been acting as though he knew more about running things than Jesse did. Two men trying to lead made for an inefficient fighting unit. There would be no more of that the next time Jesse rode.

Jesse James finished tying a tomato plant to a stake and decided to call it a day. As he stood up from the garden he noticed the two men on horseback at the side of the house. A sudden panic seized him, and he wished that he had not left his guns inside. Then he took a closer look, and he saw that the riders were Bob and Charlie Ford. He walked over to them, shaking his head. "My, my, don't you boys look fine."

"Good to see you, Jesse," Charlie said.

Bob just smiled.

"Nice-lookin' duds you got there. Horses too."

"You need good mounts for pullin' jobs," Bob said.

"Always said that myself. Things must be goin' pretty good for you fellas."

"You know how it is," Charlie said.

"Coupla things we did paid off real well." Bob Ford leaned down and stroked his horse's neck.

"We'll talk about it after a while," Jesse said. "It's time for supper. I hope you boys'll stay."

"Much obliged," Charlie said.

"Well," Jesse said. "Tie up your horses and come on. I got some things I want to talk to y'all about anyway."

"That's what we're here for." Bob Ford smiled at his brother as Jesse walked toward the house.

Jesse had prepared Beth and Zee for the Fords' arrival, so the atmosphere at the dinner table was at least civil. But once the small talk about little Jesse, Mrs. Samuel, Frank, and life in St. Joseph had ended, there was little more to say. No one was going to ask the Fords how *their* family was, and even Charlie Ford had enough tact to stay away from the subjects of Northfield, the Pinkertons, or Ed Miller.

After a particularly long moment of silence, Jesse said, "You boys gettin' enough food?"

Both Fords had a mouthful, but both nodded.

"Zee," Jesse said, "give 'em a little more grits." He grinned at the brothers. "I was pretty rough on these fellas a while back. Hope the food'll make up for it."

"The way they're eatin' I expect it will," Beth said, staring at her plate.

As Zee dished up the grits, Bob Ford looked at Jesse. "We heard you were thinkin' about a bank in Kansas."

Beth looked at Jesse.

Jesse looked at Zee as she sat down once again. "We don't discuss business at the table, boys."

"Sorry," Bob Ford said.

Charlie Ford finished his grits in three bites, then leaned back and rubbed his stomach. "I'm full up." He smiled at Zee. "Real good vittles, ma'am."

"Thank you, Mr. Ford. I appreciate the compliment." She looked back at her plate.

"You're a mighty lucky man, Jesse," Charlie said, nodding at Zee. "That woman can really throw on a meal."

"That's right." Jesse noticed that Bob had finished eating too. "How'd you boys like a drink?"

Charlie grinned. "Sounds good, don't it, Bob?"

Bob nodded.

"Why don't y'all go in the parlor and pour yourselves one," Jesse said. "I'll be right in, then we can get down to business."

The Ford brothers stood up and started out of the room.

"Charlie!" Jesse said.

Charlie whirled around, a look of panic on his face. Jesse reached out and pulled away the napkin that Charlie was wearing like a bib.

"That's better," Jesse said.

Jesse went over and rubbed his son's head as the Fords disappeared into the parlor. Zee walked past him with a stack of dishes and did not look his way.

"You feelin' okay?" he asked.

"She ain't real fond of the company," Beth said.

Zee turned around in the kitchen and looked at Jesse. "Don't worry none, Zee. We're just talkin' things over." Zee's skeptical look did not change.

"Hey," Jesse said. "That was real nice, the way you fixed dinner."

"Don't you forget it," Zee said, smiling at last.

"I won't."

In the parlor, Bob Ford took a sip of whiskey and stared at his brother. "We can't wait no longer."

"I don't know," Charlie whispered. "It don't feel right. I just don't know, Bob. There ain't no good rushin' things."

Beside Bob Ford a sampler that read "GOD BLESS OUR HOME" hung on the wall. Not far away, on a peg, hung Jesse James' guns. "He ain't wearin' no gun," Bob said.

Charlie looked over his shoulder, then whispered again. "He might be carryin' a hideout. Yeah, I'll bet he is. He knows, Bob. I know he knows. Jesus, we better think about this."

Bob Ford shook his head and walked toward the back of the room where the whiskey was. He smiled at Jesse as the famous outlaw walked into the room.

"Pour me one, Bob."

"Sure thing, Jesse."

Jesse walked right up to Charlie Ford and smiled. "You looked spooked, Charlie."

Charlie thought his knees might buckle. "Like hell," he said. "Nothin' spooks me. You know that, Jesse. It's just that the last time didn't end real friendly."

Bob handed Jesse a drink.

"Thanks, Bob." He turned back to Charlie and raised his hand in dismissal. "Forget all that. What's done is done. Future's what counts. What I'm thinkin' about is the Platte City Bank. Gonna be a real big one."

The Ford brothers exchanged glances. "We ain't too sure," Bob said.

Jesse took a drink of whiskey. "Why not?"

"I don't know," Charlie said. "That last one was—"

"You're a hard man to do business with, Jesse," Bob said.

Charlie nodded. "You ain't real easy on boys like us."

Jesse shrugged, then looked around the room, his eyes coming to rest on the sampler. "I told ya, sometimes I lose my head a bit. But I'll make it up to the both of you this time out. That sampler straight?"

"What'd you say?" Charlie asked.

"I think it's crooked." Jesse turned his back to the Fords and walked over to the far wall. He stood on a chair and began adjusting the sampler. "I really like this old thing," Jesse said. "Ma made it for our wedding day."

Bob Ford pulled out his pistol and took aim at Jesse. Charlie Ford took out his gun, then moved back behind his brother.

"How does that look?" Jesse asked.

"Looks real good." Bob Ford smiled. "I shot Jesse James," he said. He fired twice. Jesse went up on his toes, and his fingers touched the ceiling before he toppled to the floor in a lifeless heap.

Zerelda Mimms James burst through the parlor door. "What's going . . ." Her mouth hung open as she stared at Jesse for a moment. "Oh, God!" she screamed. "Mercy! You've shot him!" She ran to Jesse and hurled herself on his body, then cradled his bloody head on her breast. "You've killed him!" she cried, and she stared in hatred at Bob and Charlie Ford.

Still holding their revolvers, the Fords ran out the door, mounted their horses, and galloped away from the house of Jesse James.

30

When Frank James received the news of Jesse's death, he kept reading the message over and over again. Zee had sent a note with a courier: Jesse had been shot in the back by the cowardly Fords; Jesse's mother had been notified; the funeral would be in St. Joseph, the burial outside of Independence; they would all understand if Frank couldn't make it. "Tell them I'll be there," Frank told the courier after a few minutes.

"I'm real sorry, Mr. Woodson," the man said, then mounted his horse and headed back toward St. Joseph.

"I reckon I am too." Frank walked out to the back porch of Adam Ralston's home and sat down on a rocker that faced the spacious yard. He felt shocked, not sorry, and after a few minutes of rocking back and forth, he experienced such a profound feeling of relief that he thought he might float away. After a while he chided himself for not feeling more grief, but he knew that Jesse had put himself beyond that emotion, at least where Frank was concerned. By trying to raise himself above human limitations, Jesse had at last cheated himself of a human response to his death. That's probably the way he would have wanted it, Frank thought. To be mourned as an institution rather than as a man.

Frank rocked for two more hours, and when he finally rose to go into the house, he thought he had put the past behind him. He also felt that he had figured out what the future course of his life would be. That night at dinner, after he had told the Ralston family about Jesse's demise, he said, "I'm gonna turn myself in."

No one said anything.

"It's the only way I can make it clean for myself," Frank said. "I'm sorry, Annie."

She stared at him for a moment, shrugged, then looked back at her plate. "You have to do what you have to do, Frank. But doesn't that mean they'll hang you or put you in prison for the rest of your life?"

"I'd better clear the table." Mrs. Ralston stood up and began to gather the dishes.

"Don't get ahead of yourself, Annie," Adam Ralston said. He put his elbow on the table and rested his chin on his fist. "No one's going to hang Frank James, I know that for a fact." He grinned at his son-in-law. "I don't even think he'll spend that much time in jail. Maybe no time at all."

"What makes you say so?" Frank asked.

With his finger, Adam Ralston traced a circle on the tablecloth. "Don't know if there's twelve men in Missouri who'd vote to put you away."

"I don't know about that," Frank said. "Guess I'll just have to take my chances."

"Guess so," Adam Ralston said. "Frank, let's go have a brandy." He stood up. "Excuse us, Annie. I won't keep your husband for long."

"Please don't," she said as the two men started for the study.

"I think you're making the right decision, Frank." Adam Ralston exhaled a geyser of cigar smoke toward the ceiling.

"I sure hope so," Frank said.

"You're not worried about hangin', are you?"

"Not at all," Frank said. "Years are the only thing I'm worried about. I probably ain't got that many left."

"How many you have left is the Lord's concern," Adam Ralston said. "But how many you spend in prison is the concern of men. I think the newspapers might help us out, especially now that Jesse's dead and the Youngers are spending their lives in a Minnesota prison."

"I don't know," Frank said. "Folks might not be all that friendly anymore."

Adam Ralston shrugged. "Time was I would've shot you myself." He took a sip of brandy. "But that's because you ran off with my daughter. I think a lot of Missouri folks are going to be real sad about Jesse James dying, especially after they find out he was shot in the back. They may be sad enough about him to let you go."

Frank really hadn't thought about it. "I hope you're right," he said. "Both for my sake and for Annie's. I didn't mean to bring no shame on her."

"She'll be all right. Frank, you go ahead and turn yourself in. I know some pretty important men in Missouri. I'll see what I can do for you."

"I appreciate it," Frank said.

"Got something else I want to mention."

"Go ahead." Here comes the hitch, Frank thought.

"An uncle of mine died a while back," Adam Ralston said. "Left me a little spread over near Excelsior Springs."

"Pretty country," Frank said.

"Good farming country."

"That's right." Frank swirled his brandy nervously.

"Left me eighty acres."

"Good size," Frank said.

"Makes money without me being there."

"I'd say that was pretty good."

"Frank?" Adam Ralston took a puff on his cigar, then rolled it between his thumb and fingers.

"Yes sir."

"If you come through this all right, I'd like to give that farm to you and Annie."

"You . . ."

"I figure you don't want to hang around here all your life."

Frank said nothing.

"I know you didn't do too well down there in Tennessee, but I reckon that wasn't your fault."

"I didn't know what I was doin'," Frank said.

"Like I said, you can make money off this place without even working. But I expect you'd want to work, and with Annie helping out you could have a right prosperous little farm."

"I'm much obliged, sir." Frank shrugged. "I don't know what else to say."

"Nothin' else *to* say," Adam Ralston said. "Farm'll keep till you take care of your other business. Now I reckon you better go talk to your wife. Don't want her mad at me."

Frank stood up. "If they let me go, I'll try not to make you regret givin' us the farm."

"Don't think I'll have to." Adam Ralston turned in his swivel chair to face some papers on his desk.

Frank James found Annie on the back-porch loveseat. Without a word, he sat down and put his arm around her. She leaned against him, and they sat silently for a while, watching the stars. Frank was shaken by his good fortune, not only because of the offer of Adam Ralston's farm, but because he had the forgiveness of his wife and the acceptance of a family that had not tried to smother him beneath a blanket of guilt and shame. "Beautiful night, ain't it, Annie?"

He felt her head nod in the darkness. "Frank, don't tell me nothin' good if you don't think it'll be the truth."

"Like what?" he asked.

"About not going to prison and all."

"I wouldn't do—"

"I'm scared, Frank."

He bowed his head. "Me too."

"Do you have to turn yourself in?"

"I don't want to spend the rest of my life lookin' over my shoulder for Pinkerton men." He squeezed her tightly. "Don't reckon you do either."

"That's true," she said.

"I think it'll work out easier this way. All around."

"If you say so, Frank. Actually I'm kind of proud of you for doin' it."

He pulled away and looked at her in the darkness. "Why, thank you, Annie."

"And Daddy seems to think it'll be all right."

"He's a wise man." Frank proceeded to tell her about the farm, and for a while they chatted and made plans and shared a few bittersweet memories about their time in Tennessee. They even talked about the possibility of having children, a subject Frank would not discuss when he was an outlaw. "Well," Frank said, "if I get a short sentence we might have a pretty good life."

"Wherever they send you, I'll come and live close by."

Frank James leaned against his wife and nearly dozed off. Finally he shook himself alert. "I reckon I better go upstairs and pack," he said. "I'd like to get out of here before sunup."

"I'm going with you," Annie said.

"No," Frank said. "You don't need to do that."

"I know I don't need to. I want to be with you, Mr. Frank James."

"Why, thank you, Annie." He stood up and pulled her to him. "I'm much obliged."

He started toward the house, but she grabbed his arm. "Frank?"

"What is it?"

"I have to say one thing."

"Go ahead and say it."

"Frank, I don't want you to take this wrong, because I feel sorry for you and Zee and your ma. But I'm relieved that Jesse's gone."

Frank shook his head, saying nothing.

"Frank, you're not mad at me, are you?"

"No, Annie," he said.

"I wanted to get it off my chest. I hope you know what I mean."

"I do, Annie." He put his arm around her and they walked into the house. "I surely do."

31

Across the street from Sidenfaden's Funeral Emporium in St. Joseph, Missouri, Jacob Rixley, Pinkerton man, leaned against a post and watched the seemingly endless line of mourners file in to pay their respects to the corpse of Jesse James. He did not feel that it was incumbent on himself to be there. Frank James had surrendered to him the previous night, and he was now acquainted with all the actors in the drama of the James/Younger Gang. He did not deem it proper to say anything to Jesse's mother or widow, and he had no desire to face down their accusatory stares.

He had said his goodbyes to Jesse James the day before. He had saved his viewing of the famous outlaw until he had been properly done up for burial, and then Jacob Rixley had ordered old Sidenfaden out of the embalming room and had a private audience with the long rider's corpse. He said no words of farewell. He simply stared at Jesse, occasionally looking around the room and remembering his long chase, acutely aware of how a single event or an assignment in one's job could turn into something momentous, something that altered one's life forever. At last he had touched Jesse's head with his hand, then run his thumb along the outlaw's brow. He had picked up the cold and rocklike hand and held it in his own for at least a minute. Yes, he had thought, Jesse James is quite dead.

Inside the funeral parlor, Zerelda Samuel sat in a wicker chair next to Beth Mimms (Zee had chosen to remain behind a curtain, out of the public eye), watching the crowd of devoted mourners. She had shed all her tears during the past couple of days, and had rallied her strength for those who had come to see her son lying in state. Stoically, she watched them all, looking into the eyes of those who looked at her and nodding slightly to the gentlemen who tipped their hats.

At twilight, when the last of the mourners had left the chapel, Carl Reddick of the New York *Herald* came up and introduced himself to Mrs. Samuel. "I'd like to ask you a few questions," he said. "Please tell me if it's not a good time."

"I'm feeling a bit tired," she said.

Reddick gave her his most sincere look. "It's for the public, ma'am. They want to know, and we want to get the facts right."

She nodded. "A few questions, then."

"What's your full name, Mrs. Samuel?"

"Zerelda Cole Samuel," she said. "My husband Robert James died in California. My second husband was called Reuben Samuel."

"Where did you and Mr. Samuel live?"

"Clay County, Missouri. But don't you know all that?"

Reddick finished jotting on his pad. "I want to get it exactly right. Are you the mother of Jesse James?"

"I am."

Reddick nodded toward the coffin. "And you recognize that to be the body of your son over there?"

"Yes, I do."

"No doubt about it?"

She gave Reddick a strange look.

"Some people have been saying that it's not really Jesse James at all."

Zerelda Samuel shook her head and sighed. "Would to God they were right."

"Thank you, Mrs. Samuel." Reddick nodded and moved over to the other chair, where Beth Mimms sat with her hands in her lap. "It must break your heart to see Jesse James lying there," Reddick said.

Beth looked at him for a moment. "Jesse dyin' wasn't unexpected," she said. "But that don't make it any easier. I'll tell you about my heart, mister. It's eight hundred miles away, locked up in Jim Younger's cell at Stillwater Prison."

"I'm sorry, ma'am," Carl Reddick said.

Frank James stood up from the chair where he'd been sitting beside Zee and Annie just as a man carrying a bowler hat in his hand pushed through the semitransparent curtain. He looked directly at Zee. "Mrs. James?"

She nodded.

"Excuse me. My name is Philip Berryman." He handed Zee his card. "I've already presented a very successful tour of the mortal remains of Charles Guiteau, the man who assassinated President Garfield. I'd make it worth your while if you'd let me do the same with Jesse."

"Get out," Frank said.

Berryman looked at Frank, then back at Zee.

"I won't tell you twice," Frank said.

Berryman hesitated only a moment before disappearing.

Frank turned to Zee. "I wish I could do something to comfort you."

Zee shook her head. "I don't need it, Frank. I got my vision of Jesse that I carry in my mind." She gave Frank a wistful smile. "I like to think of him leadin' y'all like a band of heroes ridin' from town to town."

Frank looked at her for a moment, not sure of what to say. "Well, you might not see it that way if you'd've been there."

"I know you had some hard times," Zee said. "Cold and wet at night and all. But you endured it. And that makes you better in my eyes." Zee stared at the curtain that hung between herself and her husband's corpse. "Band of heroes."

Frank gave Annie a look and shook his head. "I guess it's just hard thinkin' of people you rode with in that kind of special light."

It was as though Zee hadn't heard him. "Band of heroes," she said. "Ridin' from town to town, train to train." She turned and looked up at Frank. "Guess you'll be goin' out to hunt down them Ford brothers."

"I'm done with that."

"Jesse would've hunted them down if they'd shot you, Frank."

"I expect he would've," Frank said. "But I ain't Jesse. I turned myself in, Zee. I'm goin' back to Independence handcuffed to a Pinkerton man."

Zee stood up. "I better go look to your ma and my sister."

Frank grabbed her arm. "Zee, the Fords ain't gonna last long. Somebody's gonna show up who'll want to shoot the men who shot Jesse James."

Zee eyed him coldly. "You satisfied with that?"

"I reckon I am." Frank nodded. "I'm past all those dreams, Zee."

"Well, I ain't." She turned to go.

"Jesse is too," Frank said.

Zee walked through the curtain as though she hadn't heard him.

Jacob Rixley shook his head and smiled as he saw Carl Reddick walking toward him from the funeral parlor. "Did you get an interview with the ghost?" Rixley said.

"Now, now," Reddick said.

"Guess you got everybody else."

"I wish." Reddick shrugged. "Couldn't get to the brother or the wife. But I guess I got enough."

"You can go back home."

"That's how it looks. At least till Frank James' trial. But I might even send somebody else for that one. Trials bore me, and that's a fact."

"Speaking of facts," Rixley said, "are you going to print any in that paper of yours?"

"I'm not real sure what they are." Reddick smiled. "Might have to spice up some of these stories a little. That's what people want to read."

"Some people," Rixley said. "Be seeing you, Mr. Reddick. I've got to go pick up my prisoner."

Reddick twirled the end of his mustache, then hollered after Rixley, "Don't let him rob that train back to Independence."

32

As Frank James shifted his weight from one leg to the other, his manacled arm slipped, jerking Jacob Rixley toward him. The Pinkerton man looked at Frank in panic, his free hand going for his gun. "Don't worry," Frank said. "I ain't goin' nowhere."

"I know it." Rixley exhaled in relief. "Just spooked me is all."

The funeral train was now in deep woods, and the trees were so close that Frank could almost reach out and touch them. Small pools of sunlight lay on the lush green forest floor, and the leaves of the trees were dappled by rays that filtered through the canopy. Frank imagined desperate horsemen skirting trees as they raced to avoid the law, then he blinked and brought himself back to reality. "Funny thing," he said.

"What's that?" Rixley asked.

"All the world likes an outlaw. For some damn reason they remember 'em."

Rixley nodded. "Longer than they remember lawmen, that's for sure."

A short time later they reached a small clearing where a slight man in a battered hat and torn overalls leaned on a hoe in a patch of knee-high corn. Frank gazed down at the farmer, wondering how many times the railroads and banks had bilked him of his lands and money. Their eyes met and locked momentarily, and during that brief instant the farmer removed his hat. Frank James closed his eyes and nodded, then turned his head toward the front of the train.

"Think you and your boys helped that man a lot?" Rixley asked.

"You know we didn't." Frank moved his arm and felt the manacle's pressure on his wrist once again. "But I reckon we gave him some dreams, and that's more than the railroads did. A man like that needs more than himself to believe in. Otherwise he couldn't do what he's doin'."

Gradually the woods thinned and fell away, and before long the train was chugging through the rolling prairie hills. Not far from the tracks a couple of boys, probably just into their teens, appeared over a rise on galloping horses. They raced the train for half a mile, then waved casually at Frank and Rixley before climbing another hill and disappearing. Frank stared at the vacant horizon for a moment. He was waiting for the riders to reappear, and his heart suddenly pounded at the recollection of the first time he had topped a hill and ridden down on a train. He closed his eyes and saw himself and Jesse, Jim, Bob, and Cole thundering along in their new dusters, long riders in their prime. But when his eyes were open he saw nothing but the prairie grass undulating gently in the wind.

TOWERING ADVENTURE
BY THE AUTHOR OF
HIGH EMPIRE

CLYDE M. BRUNDY

GRASSLANDS

A former riverboat gambler comes West to stake
a land claim when the only deeds are carried in a
holster—and signed with lead. His name is Will
Cardigan and his story, and that of his children
and his children's children, is boldly etched across
seven decades, from horse to helicopter, gunplay
to graft. Interwoven are three great loves, a blazing
vendetta, and a monumental disaster that forces
the Cardigan family to pay the price of empire
on the vast Colorado plains.

Avon 🔷 75449 $2.50